THE TOMB OF GENGHIS KHAN

A James Acton Thriller

Also by J. Robert Kennedy

James Acton Thrillers

The Protocol	*Pompeii's Ghosts*	*Wrath of the Gods*
Brass Monkey	*Amazon Burning*	*The Templar's Revenge*
Broken Dove	*The Riddle*	*The Nazi's Engineer*
The Templar's Relic	*Blood Relics*	*Atlantis Lost*
Flags of Sin	*Sins of the Titanic*	*The Cylon Curse*
The Arab Fall	*Saint Peter's Soldiers*	*The Viking Deception*
The Circle of Eight	*The Thirteenth Legion*	*Keepers of the Lost Ark*
The Venice Code	*Raging Sun*	*The Tomb of Genghis Khan*
	Wages of Sin	

Special Agent Dylan Kane Thrillers

Rogue Operator	*Black Widow*
Containment Failure	*The Agenda*
Cold Warriors	*Retribution*
Death to America	*State Sanctioned*

Delta Force Unleashed Thrillers

Payback	*The Lazarus Moment*
Infidels	*Kill Chain*
	Forgotten

Templar Detective Thrillers

The Templar Detective
The Templar Detective and the Parisian Adulteress
The Templar Detective and the Sergeant's Secret
The Templar Detective and the Unholy Exorcist
The Templar Detective and the Code Breaker

Detective Shakespeare Mysteries

Depraved Difference
Tick Tock
The Redeemer

Zander Varga, Vampire Detective

The Turned

THE TOMB OF
GENGHIS KHAN

A James Acton Thriller

J. ROBERT KENNEDY

ISBN: 9781998005413

First Edition

10 9 8 7 6 5 4 3 2 1

For Deniz and Alex.

THE TOMB OF

GENGHIS KHAN

A James Acton Thriller

"The greatest happiness is to vanquish your enemies, to chase them before you, to rob them of their wealth, to see those dear to them bathed in tears, to clasp to your bosom their wives and daughters."

Genghis Khan

"I am the flail of God. Had you not created great sins, God would not have sent a punishment like me upon you."

Genghis Khan

PREFACE

There are many variations on the notion, however the most famous quotation is 'History is written by the victors.' In 1227 AD, the leader of the Mongol Empire, Genghis Khan, died at the age of 65. This is historical fact that few dispute. What is disputed is how he died. Those who revered him, generally agreed he died from a wound he received in glorious battle.

A fitting end to one of the most brutal warriors of all time, responsible for the deaths of perhaps 40 million people.

Second only to his thirst for blood was his legendary, almost mythic, sexual appetite, with as many as 16 million descendants attributed to him.

Legend has it that every night he demanded a beautiful virgin be brought to him, one who belonged to his most recently conquered foe. Is it then so hard to believe that one might have fought back, and perhaps even bested him?

There is a legend that says this very thing did happen, though as we know, history is written by the victors, and those who tell this story were certainly victims, not victors.

Yet if their story isn't true, why was a Mongolian river, known at the time as the Yellow River, renamed Khatun Gol?

The River of the Princess.

Mongolia

Present Day

Archaeology Professor James Acton cursed as his wife spun in her seat to see what he had just spotted in his rearview mirror, silhouetted against the moonlit sky. A helicopter, mere feet off the pavement, racing toward them on the lonely, barren road they had been traveling for almost two hours.

And judging by its weapons pods, it wasn't civilian.

It was straight out of a Rambo movie.

It's gotta be a Hind.

Russian made, big, brutal, and obviously Mongolian military.

He pressed harder on the accelerator.

"You're going to try and outrun them?" Archaeology Professor Laura Palmer's voice was filled with incredulity. And he didn't blame her. It was a stupid move. He eased up on the gas.

"What should I do?"

She stared at him for a moment, as uncertain as he was. "Stop before they shoot?"

He sighed, nodding in agreement as he eased off the gas, slowly bringing them to a stop as the massive machine swept over them, banking hard to the right before landing a couple of hundred yards ahead of them. Troops poured from its innards, weapons raised as they surrounded their car, orders shouted at them in Mongolian, a language of which neither of them had an inkling of understanding.

"Do you think they're going to kill us?"

Acton frowned as he stared at the soldiers, raising his hands, resisting the urge to take hers in his one last time, lest someone think he was reaching for a gun.

And he cursed at himself, for they had both been right.

This had been a colossally stupid move.

And now they might pay the ultimate price for it.

Tangut Empire, Western Xia

August 17, 1227 AD

Mutukan roared as he leaned forward in his saddle, his sword extended in front of him, the reins gripped tightly in his other hand. His master, the great Genghis Khan, was slightly ahead, leading the charge as he always did when afforded the opportunity, a formidable warrior still, despite his advanced age.

The man was an awe-inspiring sight, fearless in his intensity, beyond courageous, filled with a determination that suggested he knew nothing could stop him, nothing could hurt him.

That he would never die.

It had him wondering about his master's visit with the Taoist monk rumored to possess an elixir of immortality. Had he provided the Khan with it? Was he now immortal, and was that why he had no fear?

He dismissed the idea as someone shouted a warning of incoming arrows. He had been with the Khan since long before that meeting, and

5

the bravery had always been there. The Khan simply feared nothing, no one. There was no enemy that could defeat him if he were leading the charge.

And today's enemy would be no exception. The Tangut had crossed the line yet again, and this time they were to be shown no mercy. Total loyalty was demanded should autonomy within the empire be desired. The Khan recognized that his empire was simply too vast to control everything himself, so should an enemy capitulate and swear allegiance—which included providing troops should they be needed—then they were left alone. Should they refuse, they were slaughtered. And should they betray their allegiance later, the results were often worse.

Disloyalty would never be tolerated.

When the Tangut had refused to provide soldiers for the campaign against the Khwarezmia, it had been the final straw, and today they would pay the ultimate price. He ducked, raising his shield against the thousands of arrows inbound, then resumed the charge, unscathed, though too many of his brothers had been struck.

As had been the Khan.

He urged his horse on faster, yet his leader didn't slow. Instead, Mutukan shook his head in wonder as the arrow, embedded in his master's thigh, was snapped off, the rest forgotten as blood trickled down the Khan's leg, any pain ignored, any concern, if it existed at all, hidden.

He was a living god, and his men would do anything for him, including sacrificing themselves should he ask them.

The Tangut army lay ahead, scores already breaking ranks as the massive Mongol horde descended upon them. Death was certain, defeat inevitable, and as he swung his sword, defending his master's right flank, he reveled in the blood, in the carnage, in the cries of those dying around him, begging for mercy, pleading for forgiveness.

But no quarter would be shown today, for his master's thirst for revenge appeared unquenchable, and his words echoed in Mutukan's head.

"I am the flail of God. Had you not created great sins, God would not have sent a punishment like me upon you."

And today, whichever god had sent them, had unleashed a punishment that would soak the ground with blood for years to come.

Ulaanbaatar, Mongolia

Present Day, Two Days Earlier

Arban Namjiliin careened around the corner, the laws of physics taking over as he skidded hard, slamming into a parked car, the engine cutting out. He didn't bother trying to restart it, instead throwing the door open and sprinting into a nearby alleyway as those pursuing him caught up, tires squealing as they came to a halt.

He ducked around a corner, desperately searching for somewhere to hide, and spotted a doorway. He grabbed the handle and relief swept over him as it opened. He stepped inside, shoving the door closed as quickly and as quietly as he could, then looked for a means of escape.

And cursed.

There were no other doors, not even a window.

He grabbed his phone as he crouched against the door, the shouts of his pursuers growing louder, then typed the text message he had been planning for hours, sighing with relief that he finally had a signal, the message sent to the one man in the world whose number he had in his phone, and who just might be able to help him.

Archaeology Professor James Acton.

Milton Residence

St. Paul, Maryland

"There should be a law against that."

Professor James Acton wholeheartedly agreed with his best friend and boss, Dean of St. Paul's University Gregory Milton. "Absolutely. It should be a crime to cancel a series on a cliffhanger. And they wonder why so many shows fail in their first season. I mean, I don't bother watching anything new anymore, because I'm afraid they're just going to cancel it on me and piss me off."

"So, you're the problem."

Acton regarded his wife, Professor Laura Palmer. "I am?"

"Well, too many people think like you do, so too many of you don't watch the new shows, so they end up failing. It's a self-fulfilling prophecy."

Milton's wife Sandra laughed. "She's got you there, Jim."

Acton gave his wife the stink eye briefly. "Aren't you supposed to be on my side?"

"I always am, darling, if you're right."

"Well, we both know I'm always right."

She rolled her eyes. "Oh, sure, when have you ever made the wrong decision?"

He gave her a toothy smile. "Never!" He turned back to Milton, his best friend more likely to be on his side. "Like, how many series have the networks canceled on us, leaving us hanging? And they're usually the best ones that have story arcs. Canceling a show like Law and Order is one thing. The stories are episodic. Cancel a show like The Terminator or Lois and Clark, where there's a continuing storyline, and you piss people off. You alienate them."

Milton's head bobbed as he took another sip of beer. "You're preaching to the choir, brother. I was pissed when they canceled V! I mean, come on! If they know they're going to cancel something, they should have to do a wrap-up episode. Like Firefly!"

Acton drained his beer then jabbed a finger at Milton. "I can't believe they canceled Firefly! Whoever did that should be fired. But at least they put out that movie Serenity and gave us a bit of a sendoff."

Laura rolled her head toward Sandra. "You do realize these two will go on about this for the next two hours if we don't stop them."

Sandra laughed. "We are two lucky women, aren't we?"

Laura patted Acton on the arm. "It's hard to tell sometimes."

Acton chuckled. "Okay, fine, what would you two like to talk about?"

"Did you see the Bachelor last night?"

Acton and Milton both leaned back in their chairs, their bodies rigid planks as they both executed exaggerated groans.

Laura laughed, smacking his shoulder. "Just kidding, you bloody fool. You know I hate that crap."

Sandra agreed. "Me too. Now, the Bachelorette, that's an entirely different story."

Laura was about to say something Acton was certain he'd find horrifying, when his phone vibrated on the table with a message. He swiped his thumb and his eyes widened as he read it, then shot wide. He sat up straight as he realized it might not be the hoax he thought as he saw who it was from.

Laura picked up on his change in mood, turning toward him. "What is it?"

"It's a message from Arban Namjiliin. He was at the university a few years ago on exchange."

Milton's head bobbed. "Yeah, I remember him. I approved the funding. Mongolian, wasn't he?"

Acton nodded, holding up his phone. "He just sent me this. 'Professor, I'm in trouble. I don't know who to trust. I think they're going to kill me.'"

Sandra gasped and Laura's jaw dropped. Laura leaned closer to get a better look at the message. "Is that it? Does he say who?"

Acton shook his head. "No, that's it."

"Call him back," urged Sandra.

He was about to do just that when he paused.

"What?" asked Laura.

"Well, if he could call, he would have. Mongolia probably has horrendous cellphone service. He texted for a reason." He tapped out a message, sending it, and waited, his breath held, when a small red circle appeared indicating the message had failed to get through. "No go." He tried twice more before giving up.

Milton set his beer aside. "We need to tell someone."

Acton agreed. "But who?"

"His government? His place of employment?"

Acton shook his head. "He said he didn't know who he could trust. For all we know it's his government or employer that wants him dead."

Sandra frowned. "If it's his government..."

Acton knew what Sandra didn't want to vocalize. If the Mongolian government wanted him dead, then there was nothing they could do to help him. He was a Mongolian citizen, in Mongolia. His racing mind paused. "Wait, we don't even know where he is."

Laura gestured toward the phone. "What's the country code on the number?"

Acton brought it up. "976."

Milton turned his head. "Alexa, what is Mongolia's telephone country code?"

The smart speaker quickly replied.

976.

Sandra shrugged. "I guess that proves it."

Laura shook her head. "Not really. It just proves he used his phone that is registered in Mongolia." She chewed her cheek for a moment.

"Whenever we had exchange students, we had them list family contacts back home. I assume you do the same here?"

Acton and Milton both smiled at each other. "Of course!" Milton grabbed his phone. "Rita can look that up for us."

Sandra frowned at him. "Leave that poor woman alone. It's her day off. Someone else at the office can look it up."

Milton stuck his tongue out at her as he pressed the phone to his ear. "That woman adores me, and besides, she can log in remotely to check."

"Adores you?"

"I'm an adorable guy."

Acton gave Sandra a look. "He is, you know. It's the only reason we're still friends."

"Hi, Rita, it's Greg…sorry to call on your day off, but I need you to do me a hopefully quick favor. Jim Acton is going to text you the name of a Mongolian exchange student we had a few years ago. We need his emergency contact info…yes, I'll explain later. Thanks." He ended the call and turned to his wife. "*Adores* me."

A bird was flipped. "Then maybe she'll jump up and down on you tonight, because I certainly won't be."

Milton laughed. "Why punish yourself?"

Acton snorted as he sent Arban's info to Rita Perdok, Milton's assistant of many years, and the sweetest, nicest woman one could ever meet. "She'd be horrified to hear you two talking like that about her."

Milton frowned. "You're right."

Sandra appeared contrite as well. "Sorry."

Acton chuckled. "Don't apologize to me. Apologize to her."

14

Her mouth dropped, aghast. "Then we'd *both* be mortified!"

Milton patted her hand. "You're right. We won't speak of it again." He leaned closer. "So, the jumping up and down is back on?"

She gave him the stink eye.

Milton grinned at his guests. "I think that's a yes!"

Acton's phone vibrated and he smiled. "Say whatever you want about the woman, but she's good. I have his wife's number here. Let's just hope it's not out of date." He texted back a thank you, then dialed the number, putting it on speaker so everyone could hear.

It was answered after several rings.

In Mongolian.

"Hello, is this Badma Namjiliin?"

"Yes?"

"Hello, my name is Jim Acton. Your husband, Arban, was a student of mine several years ago in the United States."

"Professor Acton?"

"Yes. He mentioned me?"

"Yes, of course, he spoke very highly of you."

"Ma'am, I received a rather disturbing text message from Arban a few minutes ago. Is he all right?"

"You heard from him?"

She sounded worried, the others leaning in as they evidently picked up on it as well.

"A single text message that indicated he was in trouble. Have you heard from him?"

"No, I'm so worried! I've tried calling the Ministry, but he doesn't answer. His supervisor doesn't answer, nor will anyone tell me where he is. I don't know what's going on, but for me to not hear from him all day is so unlike him."

"So, he's working for the government?"

"Yes." She sniffed. "Ministry of Education, Culture and Science. He was so proud to get the job. It's a good job, in his field."

"Is he in the capital?"

"Yes. Ulaanbaatar. But that's not where he spends his days, at least for the past couple of weeks."

Acton leaned closer to the phone, the connection choppy. "Where has he been working?"

"I'm not sure, all I know is it's out of the city, and something he wasn't allowed to talk to me about. He said it was very important, and an honor to have been chosen by his supervisor to participate, since he was so young and new."

Acton chewed his cheek for a moment. If they were going to give any information to the authorities, they needed more. The fact Arban was working for the government suggested a possibility that they could be who was after him, though he hoped it wasn't—for there'd be no chance for the poor kid if it were true.

"Does he do any work from home?"

"Yes, he's always on his computer."

"Do you have access?"

"No. I mean, it's sitting right here, but I don't know his password." A heavy sigh resulted in a burst of static. "Professor, I'm really worried.

If he said he's in trouble, then I don't know who to trust. For him to send a message to you must mean he doesn't know who to trust here. Is there anything you can do? Can you help him? Please?"

Laura grabbed his arm, squeezing it, and he turned to see her eyes filled with tears at the heartbreak in Badma's voice. He smiled knowingly at her.

"I'm going to make some calls. Stay by your phone. I'll call you back shortly."

"Oh, thank you so much, Professor. You really are the wonderful man my husband said."

Acton smiled. "I'll call soon. Goodbye."

"Goodbye."

He ended the call with a tap then blasted a breath through pursed lips.

"That poor woman," said Sandra. "I'd be worried sick!"

Laura agreed. "We have to help her any way we can." She patted Acton's arm. "So, who are you going to call?"

"Who do you think?"

Tangut Empire, Western Xia

August 17, 1227 AD

Mutukan's master's leg had been tended to. It was a vicious wound, though ignored by the Khan the entire time it had been treated. No pain had been shown, no concern shared. It was as if it were a mere streak of soiled skin that required nothing but a warm bath to rid himself of it.

Again, such courage.

To say he worshipped his master was an understatement. He adored him like a living god, he embodied everything a man should want to be, and had proven himself wise beyond all others.

For ruling an empire so vast required far more than cunning on the battlefield. It took administrative skills, and diplomatic skills.

And sometimes those diplomatic skills demanded difficult decisions be made.

Like those about to be.

What remained of the royal family of the defeated Tangut were on their knees, lined up for the Khan to decide their fate. The head of the family was already dead, his sons and daughters all that remained. As the Khan slowly walked the line, his men were systematically burning the city, slaughtering all the males in the capital, and taking their women as spoils of war.

But the best would be preserved for the Khan, who would choose from the most beautiful whom he would bed, the rest going to those he chose to honor for their service, reward for their bravery, or inspire to fight even harder in hopes of additional prizes of the flesh.

"Your empire is no more. Your armies vanquished. Your future erased." He stopped in front of the eldest son. "Your line is finished." He drew his sword and swung, the son's head tumbling to the floor, the gleaming stone now stained as the slain prince's brothers attempted to hide their fear unsuccessfully, his sisters sobbing. "Cowardice will not be tolerated." Another head was severed. "Disloyalty will be punished." Another, this one requiring an uncharacteristic second blow that had Mutukan concerned.

Is he growing weak?

He glanced at the leg, blood trickling onto the floor from under his pants.

He must rest!

"Your deaths will be a message to all who dare oppose me." He raised his arm to behead the final prince when he stopped, wavering slightly. Mutukan stepped forward to offer a steadying hand when the Khan grunted at him, dismissing him with a jerk of the chin.

Then finished the male bloodline of the court of Tangut.

In one stroke.

He regarded the princesses then pointed at the most beautiful. "Her."

"Yes, my master."

The Khan spun on his heel, swiftly leaving the room, a trail of blood marking his path as the other princesses, not given the honor to serve their new master, were taken away to be enjoyed by those the Khan would single out at tonight's celebratory feast.

Mutukan stepped in front of the remaining princess, staring down at her, his crotch mere inches from her face. "Look at me."

She didn't.

He grabbed her by the chin, jerking her head up. "Look at me."

She glared at him, defiance in her eyes as she trembled at what was to come.

"Your name."

"Princess Kurbelyin Goa Khatun."

He gripped her chin tighter. "You are a lucky woman, Princess. Tonight, you will serve your Khan, and should you please him, you may just live to see tomorrow."

She tore her chin away with a jerk of her head. "I would rather burn in the pits of eternal damnation than bed that pig of a man."

Mutukan raised his hand to beat the insolence from her, yet he held back. His master wouldn't be pleased if he delivered a bruised, broken woman to him. And besides, defiance was what the master liked.

A smile spread and he grabbed her chin again. "Be just like that tonight, Princess, and you *will* please him."

Unknown Location, Mongolia

Present Day

"Did you get him?"

Hendrick Stander nodded at his client, Michael Conrad, a pissant of a man if there ever was one. He was a pencil pusher from America who acted physically tough, the diminutive man likely suffering from a Napoleon complex that he overcompensated for, especially around men like Stander, whom it was obvious the man felt inferior to.

"Yes," replied Stander, his hands clasped behind his back, his posture perfect, decades of military and private security service never to be forgotten.

"I sense a but."

"He texted someone before we located him."

"Who?"

"I don't know yet. The name on the phone is James Acton. I've got my men looking into it."

Conrad rose from behind his desk and paced the room. "This isn't good. James Acton. It sounds Anglo. What would a local nobody kid be doing with a foreigner's phone number?"

"No idea. It's a stateside number. He should be easy enough to track down."

"And the message?"

Stander removed Arban's phone from his pocket and pulled up the message. "'Professor, I'm in trouble. I don't know who to trust. I think they're going to kill me.'"

Conrad cursed. "Well, if that doesn't pique someone's interest, I don't know what would. And you know what interest means. Questions. We can't afford questions." He stopped his pacing. "Okay, find this Professor Acton and eliminate him."

Stander regarded his client for a moment. This was the problem with men like Conrad. They too often were impulsive, not thinking things through. "Isn't that risky? Killing someone here is one thing, but in the US? That's something entirely different."

Conrad stepped closer, staring up at him. Stander kept his eyes forward as if the man was a drill sergeant and not to be looked at. "Do you have any idea what's at risk here? We're talking billions. Tens of billions. I don't care who has to die. When I hired you, I was told you were the man to get things done, the man I could count on to do whatever it took to protect what we've got here." Stander could see the man's face get closer, Conrad evidently on his tiptoes. "Are you that man, or was I misinformed?"

Stander stared down at Conrad, controlling his desire to snap the tiny neck. "I'm your man. You want somebody dead back in the US, then so be it. I'm just letting you know the risks."

Conrad stepped back, returning to his chair behind his desk. "I'm well aware of the risks. Seattle sent me here because I'm willing to do whatever it takes to succeed." He pointed at the door. "Now, do your job, and never question my orders again. Kill Professor Acton and anyone he may have told about the message."

Stander clicked his heels. "Yes, sir."

Acton/Palmer Residence

St. Paul, Maryland

"We might need your help."

Tommy Granger nodded at James Acton as their respective partners entered the room with a platter of homemade nachos. Laura Palmer placed the steaming mound of inauthentic Mexican cuisine on the table as Mai Trinh delivered bowls of guacamole and sour cream. Tommy's hand darted toward the food when Mai slapped it down.

"Manners!"

Tommy blushed and retreated, waiting for Laura to sit, Acton winking at his wife, always enjoying the company of the younger couple. Mai had helped save them and some friends in Vietnam from a frameup by the Vietnamese and Russian governments, and had been forced to flee to the United States. She now worked for Acton at the university, where she met Tommy Granger, a graduate student who had a knack for computers—such a knack that he had been arrested as a teenager for hacking the Department of Defense.

And it was those skills they needed.

"Do you think you can get into the computer?" asked Acton, partaking of the nachos now that everyone had settled down. Tommy tentatively reached out then stopped, glancing at Mai who rolled her eyes and gave the go ahead. He grinned and grabbed.

"If it's connected to the Internet somehow, then easily. If not, then I'll need to access it physically. Shouldn't be a problem." He crunched through a mouthful then took a drink. "I'll just go with you. I don't mind."

Laura shook her head. "Absolutely not. It could be dangerous."

Tommy shrugged. "I've gone with you before."

"Yes, but this is Mongolia. Not exactly Germany."

"But I want to help. Communications are spotty from there, and bandwidth is for sure low. Trying to connect from here will be almost useless. It would be like that old movie you had me watch, Doc, WarGames."

Acton grunted. "Hey, it was state of the art when it came out. Love that movie."

Tommy shrugged. "It was okay."

Mai dabbed the corners of her mouth with a napkin. "It would have been better if you hadn't spent the entire time tearing it apart."

Tommy turned to Acton, knowing he wouldn't get anywhere with Laura. "What if you can't reach me to help you access it? Or I can't connect from here?"

"We'll deal with it. Like Laura said, it could be dangerous. We could be dealing with dangerous people."

"Doc, you're always dealing with dangerous people. Hell, we've been shot at and I was almost killed right here on home soil." He grinned. "Frankly, no place is safe when you two are around."

Acton shook his head. The kid was right. Bad things just happened around them. Milton, his best friend, had been shot twice in the back just for helping him, Mai had nearly been killed saving them, Tommy and Mai had been kidnapped, with Tommy nearly killed.

Nobody was safe.

Yet it didn't mean he should be intentionally putting them into harm's way.

Tommy pressed on. "Your friend needs help. You need to access his computer, and you know I'm the only one who can do it. And the bottom line is, I'm willing to go."

Acton sighed, leaning back in his chair, the nachos forgotten. "I don't know. If only it wasn't Mongolia. If only we knew more." He cursed. "If only we'd heard back from Dylan."

Laura swallowed some of her creation. "He must be on an op somewhere. Incommunicado."

"I'm not surprised. But do we wait? I mean, minutes count here, don't they? It's been four hours since we received that text message this afternoon. I say you give Mary a call, book the jet, and we head there now. When we arrive, if Dylan has something for us, we can turn right around. If not, we go see Arban's wife, check out the computer, and hopefully find out who might be involved. We can then get that info to Dylan, and maybe he can help somehow."

Mai cleared her throat. "Umm, can't Dylan get that information himself? I mean, can't he go there himself?"

Acton nodded. "I'm sure he could, but he works for the CIA. He can't just drop what he's doing and pop over to Mongolia just because an old student of mine *might* be in trouble. We need something more concrete, and even then, it's unlikely our government would do anything about it."

"Then what's the point?" asked Mai. "I mean, not that I don't think he should be helped, but I mean, if there's nothing you can do with the information, then why bother?"

Acton shook his head. "No, you're forgetting one thing. Right now, we don't know who we can trust. Let's say we find out something from what's on his computer. It might let us know who is actually after him. What if it isn't the government at all? It might be some local gang, a pissed off neighbor, any number of things. If we could determine that, then we might be able to go to the local authorities and they could help."

Tommy smacked his hands together. "Then that settles it. You need access to that computer at a minimum. I'm coming with you."

Acton sighed. "If I could be sure they wouldn't be waiting for us at the airport, then maybe. But if they caught him, then they have his phone, which means they might know about the text message. If they're connected enough, they could be monitoring passenger lists of incoming flights."

Mai raised a tiny finger. "Umm, I have an idea."

27

They all turned to her. "What?" asked Laura.

"Well, I was watching a movie the other day, Catch Me If You Can, and, well, it gave me an idea."

"What?" asked Tommy, grabbing another serving of nachos.

"Well, you need us—"

Acton cut her off. "Let me stop you right there. We need Tommy, not you."

Mai squared her shoulders. "Where he goes, I go."

Tommy grinned. "She loves me."

Laura wagged a finger. "Nuh-uh. There's no way you're both coming."

Mai regarded Laura, motioning toward Acton. "Would you let him go anywhere that might be dangerous without you?"

Laura frowned. "That's not exactly a fair comparison. I've got training for these situations."

"Yes, but what are you asking of him? You need him to help on the tech side of things, not out fighting bad guys, right?"

"Your point?"

"Well, we just need to be in a hotel room, right? I mean, Tommy doesn't need to actually be in front of the computer, does he?"

Tommy nodded. "That's true, actually. Doc, if you were at the computer, I could give you a device to install that would use the local cellular network to allow me access. Cell coverage might be spotty outside the cities, but you said he lives in the capital, so it should be fine there for local connections and stable enough for me to help you from a stationary location. I wouldn't need to be in the field."

Acton chewed his cheek for a moment, his head bobbing slowly as he regarded the young man. And he was a man. He had matured rapidly over the past year, thanks in no small part to his relationship with Mai. Yet he still thought of Mai, and now Tommy, more as his children than adults. Since she had helped them in Vietnam and been forced into exile, they had become very close with her, and now Tommy as an extension of that. And the fact they couldn't have children of their own had both of them latching onto them in a perhaps too paternalistic fashion.

They were young adults, old enough to make their own decisions.

And mistakes.

He couldn't keep treating them like children that needed his protection.

Yet he also didn't need to enable them.

He sighed, turning to Laura. "What do you think?"

"I think they should both stay here. What if Arban really is in trouble and has been caught? Like you said, they might have his phone. They could be waiting for us. We could walk off that plane and be targets."

"All the more reason to take us with you," said Mai.

Laura eyed her. "How do you figure that? You'd be targets too."

Mai smiled. "You never let me tell you my idea."

29

Tangut Empire, Western Xia

August 17, 1227 AD

Fear gripped Princess Khatun as a group of women bathed her in preparation for what was to be a 'great honor' if they were to be believed. The very notion disgusted her, and what lay ahead terrified her. She was overwhelmed with grief, her stomach churning with the images of her parents' death, the beheadings of her brothers, and the impending rapes of her sisters.

Yet she hid her terror.

She hid her sorrow.

She wouldn't give these people the satisfaction.

Yet these women weren't to blame. They were slaves, like she soon would be. What would her life be after tonight? She had no intention of pleasing the murderous barbarian in his bedchambers. Whatever he did to her tonight would be against her will, from beginning to end. She would not give him any of the satisfaction he desired.

And when it was all over, and he was done with her, legend had it she would never see him again, as he preferred to change his partners nightly, unless one of his wives were accompanying him.

He's a pig.

With her mind preoccupied with her fate and that of her sisters, it took her a moment to realize those who had been attending to her had stepped back. She glanced down and gasped at the sheer robes she now wore, the finest of silks adorning her body, silks so thin they left little to the imagination.

"Now for your hair," said one of the women.

Khatun was guided into a chair and she closed her eyes as two women styled her hair in a manner she was certain was designed to please her rapist. Before long they were done, and she was shown the end result in a polished copper mirror.

She hated that she looked beautiful.

"You are ready."

She shook her head and rose. "Not yet. Where are my things?"

"What?"

"The things I was wearing when you brought me here."

The woman pointed at a table behind her and Khatun stepped over to it, selecting an item of jewelry that had been a gift from her father. She slid it into her hair. "*Now* I am ready."

The woman shook her head. "The Khan forbids any jewelry that he doesn't provide."

"The Khan wants me to please him, does he not?"

The woman frowned. "Of course."

31

"Then as a Tangut princess, I must have this one item. It was a gift from my father, and should you not permit me to wear it, I will make it clear to the Khan why I am unable to please him."

The woman's eyes bulged, and she was about to say something when a roar erupted from the other side of the draped wall of the massive tent they were in.

"Send her, now!"

Her attendants bowed deeply as they retreated, the woman in charge pointing at a heavy curtain that hung nearby, marking the entrance to the Khan's bedchambers.

And her impending rape.

Beidaihe, China

Present Day

CIA Special Agent Dylan Kane walked out of the ocean and onto the beach as naked as the day he was born, an unfortunate incident with some coral tearing off his swim trunks, and a wicked unexpected undertow carrying him off course. Heads swiveled as a ripple of shock spread among those enjoying the sun. He walked over to a young woman, her mouth agape, her eyes locked on his nether region, a towel gripped in her hand.

"May I?" he asked in perfect Mandarin.

She nodded and handed him the towel, which he wrapped around his waist.

Eliciting a slew of groans from scores of women.

And a few men.

He continued to stride through the sun worshippers, most already ignoring him as the show was now over. He stepped inside a beachside restaurant and approached one of the staff.

"I'm sorry, but all of my belongings were stolen when I was swimming. Can I use your phone?"

The young woman's eyes bulged and she bowed out several apologies as she led him to a phone. He thanked her then dialed his old buddy, Chan Chao.

"Where the hell are you?"

Kane glanced around. "Not where I'm supposed to be."

"Where are you?"

"I think Beidaihe."

"That's a public beach."

"Yup. Can you pick me up? I'm naked."

"They inserted you naked?"

"It wasn't the plan."

Chan chuckled. "How were your reviews?"

"If it weren't for the Russian judge, I'd say a solid ten-point-oh."

"You do love yourself, don't you?"

"I'm a beautiful specimen. I'm not going to deny it. Just ask your wife."

"Bah! You can have her. Sit tight, I'll be there in ten minutes. Try not to get arrested."

Kane hung up then headed for the parking lot, his feet burning on the asphalt. He spotted Chan arriving a few minutes later. He was about to climb in the passenger seat when Chan pointed a gun at him.

THE TOMB OF GENGHIS KHAN

"If your ass so much as touches my leather, I shoot you." He pointed at a bag in the back. "Your stuff. Get dressed."

"You don't think people will notice?" Kane asked as he opened the rear door.

"It's a beach. Look around you. Lots of people are changing into street clothes. None are hanging their boys out for the world to see, but you're American. They expect you to be different."

Kane slipped on a pair of underwear. "I'm sure my balls look no different than an Aussie's."

"True, but all you white guys look alike to us. You just sound different."

He perched on the edge of the rear seat and pulled on some socks then pants. "Now, when you say we all look alike, do you mean our faces, or our balls?"

Chan roared with laughter. "Both!"

Kane finished buttoning up his shirt, filled his pockets with the accouterments of being a man and a spy, then put on the CIA issued watch. He entered a coded sequence to activate it for his personal ID, then frowned when an electric pulse surged through his arm indicating a secure message.

He climbed in the passenger seat, once again ready to join polite society, and Chan slammed the car in gear, guiding them back to the hotel. "Why the insertion? Normally you just come in using your cover."

"They don't want me on any airport cameras."

"Why?"

"I could tell you but then I'd have to kill you."

Chan grunted. "Please, put me out of my misery. My wife's on hormone replacement therapy. She's as horny as a teenager." He eyed Kane. "When you're done, could you swing by and take one for the team?"

Kane laughed as he logged into the phone Chan had provided, accessing his secure messaging app. "Careful. Once she's met Little Dylan, she might not want you anymore."

Chan stared at him. "I'll give you fifty grand if you can make that happen."

Kane frowned as he read the message from his old college professor, James Acton. They had reestablished contact several years ago, and ever since, he had been forced to save the man's ass too many times. He didn't mind. Acton would—and had—done the same for him and his friends on occasion. He simply found it fascinating how much trouble the man got himself into, usually through no fault of his own.

But this time, if he indeed were in trouble, it was his own doing.

"I can't believe it."

Chan glanced at him as he guided them through the chaos that was Chinese traffic. "What?"

"Oh, an old friend is running toward the danger again." He frowned at the timestamp then quickly typed out a message and sent it.

I'll see what I can find out. Whatever you do, don't go there. Too dangerous.

"I've gotta make a call." He forwarded Acton's message to his old high school buddy, Chris Leroux, an Analyst Supervisor at the CIA, then dialed his number. He answered on the second ring.

"Hello?"

"Hey, buddy, did I interrupt anything good?"

Leroux chuckled. "Not this time, Sherrie's out with Fang. I'm at the office. I was just about to send you a message."

Kane frowned. "Let me guess. The professors are already in it up to their eyeballs?"

Leroux sighed. "So, you know."

"I know very little. He sent me a message sometime yesterday about a former Mongolian exchange student that might be in trouble. I've forwarded you the info but it's pretty scant. What have you got?"

"Some Echelon intercepts from Mongolia. Somebody there is *very* interested in Professor Acton, and already knows he's about to arrive."

Kane cursed. "What is it about those two?"

"They keep us employed, I guess."

Kane grunted. "So do the crazies. I'd rather they stayed home for a change and stopped creating work for us."

"Like that's ever going to happen."

Kane checked his watch. "Look, I'm about to go dark, so I can't help them. Can I leave this with you?"

"Consider it done."

"Thanks, buddy. Give Fang a kiss for me."

Leroux paused. "Umm, I think I'll let Sherrie do that. Fang's liable to snap my neck."

Kane grinned.

He's probably right.

Acton/Palmer Residence

St. Paul, Maryland

Willem Du Toit disabled the rather primitive alarm then listened to confirm what he already knew. The house was empty. He had watched it from his car for almost an hour, and had seen nothing, and a fake delivery to their mailbox by the door had allowed him to peek inside and see the alarm panel indicating it was enabled.

Meaning the house was indeed empty.

And that was disappointing. He had hoped to show up, put a couple of holes in this Professor Acton after some questioning, then make it appear to be a home invasion gone bad. Now, he would have to search for clues as to where he was, and either go get him, or wait for him.

And waiting could mean hours upon hours of boredom, and if there was one thing he hated, it was being bored.

He slowly strolled through the house, his expert eye taking in every detail, and he frowned at a wedding photo. Acton was married, which meant someone else lived here, and he likely told her about the text message.

Two to kill.

And with every person exposed to that information, the dead pool expanded exponentially.

A pile of mail sat nearby. He picked it up and leafed through it, most of it to James Acton, though several were for Laura Palmer. He pulled out his phone and Googled the two names together, his eyebrows shooting up as he dug deeper.

This could be a problem.

He dialed his boss, Hendrick Stander.

"Yes?"

"It's Du Toit. We've got a problem."

"What?"

"Professor Acton isn't home, but he's married to a woman named Laura Palmer. It turns out she's rich."

"How rich?"

"I don't know. Richie Rich rich. She inherited hundreds of millions when her brother died. He was some sort of tech tycoon who had sold his company. If she's got that kind of money, then she probably has connections. Killing her and her husband could prove problematic."

The front door opened and the alarm chirped.

"Someone's here. I'll call you back."

He shoved the phone in his pocket and drew his weapon, entering the hallway to find a man standing there. A man who wasn't Acton.

The new arrival's eyes bulged, his jaw dropping. "Who the hell are you?"

Du Toit raised his weapon. "Who the hell are *you?*"

The man raised his hands. "G-Greg Milton. I-I'm a friend of Jim and Laura's."

"Why are you here?"

"To-to check on their house while they're away."

Du Toit's eyes narrowed. "Where'd they go?"

"Who are you? What do you want?"

Du Toit flicked his weapon, indicating for Milton to follow him into the living room. "I'm asking the questions here." He shoved him into a seat. "Now, where'd they go?"

Milton said nothing.

He pressed his gun against Milton's forehead. "Is the answer really worth dying for?"

Milton trembled, still saying nothing. Du Toit pressed harder and Milton's shoulders slumped. "Mongolia."

Du Toit cursed then pulled out his phone, hitting redial.

Stander immediately answered. "What's going on?"

"I've got a guy here named Greg Milton. Claims to be a friend of Acton's. He says they've gone to Mongolia."

Stander cursed. "Find out everything he knows. And keep him alive. We may be able to use him as leverage."

"Will do." He ended the call then turned to Milton with a sneer. "Now, how about you and I have a conversation." He tugged at the cuffs of his gloves. "The hard way."

40

Approaching Ulaanbaatar, Mongolia

Clarice couldn't believe her bad luck. She understood part of her job was to help with the trainees, but never in her short career had she been assigned two.

And two who seemed entirely inept, as if they hadn't even taken the basic training of being a flight attendant on a private charter.

It was infuriating.

And she had little doubt what was going on.

They were friends of somebody.

They had to be. It was the only explanation for why they could be so unqualified, yet be here with her shuttling two obviously wealthy, despite all outward appearances, clients on their way to Mongolia.

Mongolia? Why of all places would you want to go there?

She had been there once before and hated it, though when she got the urgent call and an offer of time-and-a-half, she jumped at it despite her misgivings. Private charters were usually scheduled at least a day in advance, but this had been a last-minute request, so a premium was being paid. The two passengers had money, though were dressed no better than she might on a casual day lounging at home.

She immediately liked them.

Too often the rich were so full of themselves, especially the entertainers, that she could barely tolerate her job. Usually, the business people were decent, though some of them, especially the spouses and children, thought you were mere chattel, and treated you as such.

But not these two.

That was why she wanted to give them a pleasant experience, and these two morons had made that difficult the entire flight.

A flight thankfully over, the plane now landing.

Her one time here had lasted only six hours. It was a shithole with nothing to do, one of the most boring six hours she had ever spent, not even her phone working.

And this time would be worse.

Normally the plane would refuel then head off for the next client pickup. After all, this was a lease-share plane. This time, however, they would be remaining in Mongolia until the clients' business was done, and no definite departure time had been provided beyond, "It will probably just be a day or two."

Probably.

And a day or two in Mongolia would feel like a month in Dubai.

Broad smiles were exchanged as the clients disembarked, then the thankless task of cleanup began, though with these two passengers, that meant barely anything. It wasn't like Guns N' Roses in their heyday had just spent half a day partying here.

That would have been fun!

While the celebrities were usually the worst in how they treated her on board, the bands often invited her out to party with them, gave her backstage passes, and on occasion the festivities carried on in the bedroom.

It was an exciting life, if not degrading at times. There was nothing like having sex with someone the night before, then serving them and their entourage the next day with it open season for busy hands because somehow the right to grope the help had been purchased by the good time shown only hours before.

She regretted it every time.

"So, Clarice, will we see you in the bar?"

She smiled at the pilot and copilot as they left. "You can count on it." They were both cute, though the pilot was married. That didn't stop a lot of them, but the copilot, Jeff, he was single, and his ogling certainly suggested he was interested.

I can think of worse ways to spend some time in Mongolia.

Clean up was fast thanks to the trainees, and in less than an hour they were at their hotel, a cesspool by the standards she was used to, though probably upscale for Mongolia.

She decided to play nice.

"We're meeting for drinks downstairs in about half an hour. You two are welcome to join us."

The girl shook her head. "No thanks, I'm just going to stay in my room."

"Me too," said the guy.

"Suit yourselves." Clarice entered her room, slutting up just enough to not look too desperate, but enough to make it clear to Jeff that should he want to fly her friendly skies, she was available.

She stepped into the hallway in time to see the female trainee enter her counterpart's room.

Someone's a quick worker.

A flash of jealousy washed over her. What was it with white guys and Asian women? They barely spoke to each other on the plane, and already they were getting jiggy with it?

She shrugged and headed for the elevator.

Jeff better be game, because I'm horny.

Operations Center 3, CIA Headquarters

Langley, Virginia

"I'm in!"

Analyst Supervisor Chris Leroux turned in his chair, located at the center of one of the impressive operations centers at the CIA. Jampacked with enough gear and communications capability to run a sizeable war, today things were light for his team, and the only reason his boss, National Clandestine Service Chief Leif Morrison, had permitted their little surveillance operation.

And the real reason it was entertained was who the subjects were.

The country owed the professors. Big time. Based upon false intel provided by a corrupt president, Acton had been targeted by the elite Delta Force for elimination, Acton and his students put on the President's Termination List naming them all as domestic terrorists.

It was a blight on all their records, though he had no involvement in it.

Once the truth had been discovered, the wrongs were righted where possible, but too many innocents were dead.

And it meant that the Delta Force's Bravo Team had dedicated themselves to rebalancing the bad karma created, through helping Acton and whomever he was attached to, whenever and wherever possible.

And that often ended up involving him and his team, and though he barely knew the professors, he had a connection with them, especially through his best friend, Kane, that had him helping whenever possible.

Like today.

When the morons headed into danger for no apparent reason other than the fact they couldn't help themselves from helping others, no matter the risk to their own lives.

I think they count on getting bailed out.

Though that was easier said than done in a country like Mongolia, landlocked between the two hostile nations of Russia and China, with minimal tech, and piss poor communications infrastructure. It would be almost impossible to get serious boots on the ground should it become necessary, and there was precious little they could tap from here to help on the fly.

Hell, they couldn't even get a drone into position without the Chinese or Russians going apeshit and shooting it out of the sky.

The professors, for all intents and purposes, might be on their own on this one.

He turned to his team's wunderkind, Randy Child. "Took you long enough."

Child shrugged. "Hey, there was no pathway to the airport. Connection problems. We *are* talking Mongolia here, not Minnesota. It's only a couple of steps up from North Korea."

Leroux decided not to keep pressing the kid's buttons. "What have you got?"

"Not much." Child's fingers operated his keyboard furiously, information appearing on the mass of displays that curved across the entire front of the room. "Their flight arrived about an hour ago."

"Video?"

"I've got one camera in the charter terminal. Give me a sec." Some more keystrokes then a chin jutted toward the front of the room. Leroux turned to see the professors clearing the brief customs check associated with private flights, the rich and powerful rarely subjected to the annoyances the cattle were.

"Can you track them?"

"I'll do my best. We don't have great satellite coverage of that area, and they don't exactly have a lot of cameras connected to the Internet. This is going to be tough unless we can retask some satellites or get someone on the ground."

Leroux shook his head. "Not an option. The Chief approved us keeping an eye on things so long as a higher priority task doesn't come along. No assets outside of this room."

Sonya Tong, one of his senior analysts with an unhealthy crush on her boss, turned from her station. "Agent Kane is in the area, isn't he?"

Leroux faced her. "In a manner of speaking, but he's on assignment and might not be able to get there for days. For now, the professors are on their own."

Child interrupted. "Sir, I've got another Echelon intercept. I think Dean Milton is in trouble."

Tangut Empire, Western Xia

August 17, 1227 AD

There was no hiding the trembling. Princess Khatun was too terrified, despite the brave face she hoped was on display. She stood in the middle of the Khan's bedchambers, a bed only feet away covered in silks and pillows, candlelight and torches surrounding them, the floor piled with the softest of animal hides.

Any woman, any princess, would be thrilled to have a bedchamber such as this to call her own.

And that might be exactly why it was decorated so.

To make those who were about to be taken against their will comfortable.

What a high opinion he must have of himself.

"You are very beautiful, Princess."

She said nothing.

"Do you ignore your Khan's compliments?"

Again, she said nothing as he continued to circle her, taking in his prize with widening eyes. He came to a stop in front of her, his eyes boring into hers as she met his gaze, determined to let him know that despite his mastery of her body, he had none over her mind.

"I admire your courage, however useless it is." His hand darted out and he grabbed her by the throat. "No matter how much you resist, this *is* happening."

She grabbed at his hand, trying to pry it from her neck, but it was of no use. His grip was like iron, and as she gasped against the ever-tightening hold, her world drifted out of focus and she began to lose consciousness when she was abruptly released. She collapsed to the floor, gasping for breath and coughing, and as her senses returned, she recoiled, the Khan having removed his pants, his eager pride wagging in front of her face.

"Now, Princess, we do this the easy way, or the hard way." He grabbed her by the back of the head, pulling her toward him. "And so you know, I prefer the hard way."

She turned her head to the side as he pulled her closer, his flesh touching her cheek, her mouth filling with bile. He pinched her nose, forcing her to hold her breath as he laughed. She stole a glance up at him, her eyes watering, and when he tossed his head back in victory as she gasped for air, she gripped the gift from her father she had tucked in her hair and squeezed. She felt the click and pulled the end with her fingers, her thumb pressed against the sheath as she withdrew the hidden blade.

And shoved it into her rapist's scrotum, then yanked the razor sharp edge toward her as he screamed in agony.

Ending, she prayed, his reign of tyranny over women forever.

Kempinski Hotel Khan Palace

Ulaanbaatar, Mongolia

Present Day

Mai Trinh checked her phone for the umpteenth time as she paced their small hotel room. "I'm still not getting a steady signal. It keeps dropping off."

Tommy Granger, sitting cross-legged on the bed, hammered away at his keyboard, an array of equipment spread out around him including things that appeared to be mini satellite dishes. He was the geek in this relationship, and this was all Greek to her.

But she loved him dearly.

This was despite the fact he was nothing like the man she had pictured marrying her entire life as a girl in Vietnam. Of course, living there, she had never imagined falling in love with a white guy. Sure, there were the fantasies about being swept away by some movie star, but those were girlish infatuations. She had just assumed she'd find a nice Vietnamese boy, fall in love, get married, have children, grow old together, and pass away within days of the other.

The standard naïve life plan.

Little could she have known she'd be witness to the murder of a head of state while giving a tour of a museum to the professors, then be drawn into an international conspiracy to frame America for the murder. She had done the right thing then, completely disrupting her life in the process, just as she was doing the right thing now.

Though she doubted gunmen would burst through their door any time soon.

Her plan had worked.

She had seen it in the movie. If you wear the uniform and act the part, nobody questions you. And with Laura's connections, she got them on as crew trainees, and the rest was child's play.

Tommy threw his arms up in victory. "I'm connected!"

"Won't it just drop like mine?"

He shook his head. "No, I'm connected differently."

"How?"

He gave her a look. "Do you really want to know?"

She chuckled. "No."

Tommy dialed his phone, putting it on speaker. Acton answered.

"Hello?"

"Hi, Doc, it's us. I'm connected. We should be good to go when you are."

"Good work. We've just checked into our hotel. We'll be heading to Arban's house in a couple of minutes. Remember what we said. You two don't leave that hotel room for any reason. *Any*. Order room service as much as you want, and try to take it easy on the dirty movies."

Tommy shifted uncomfortably and Mai blushed.

They both enjoyed a good blue movie now and then.

"Umm, I doubt they have those in Mongolia," came Tommy's meek reply.

Acton laughed. "I'm just joking, Tommy. We'll have to work on that sense of humor."

Tommy flushed even more. "Okay, Doc, you got me on that one. Oh, don't forget the interface I gave you. Just plug it into a USB port and it should give me full access to the computer."

"Yup, I've got your little kit in my hand. We're leaving now. You should hear from us within an hour."

"Good luck!" called Mai.

"To all of us."

Acton/Palmer Residence

St. Paul, Maryland

Milton gasped as he was punched in the stomach yet again. The only mercy was that he hadn't taken another blow to his face. His nose was broken at least ten minutes ago, blood dripped from his bulging lips, and he feared for his vision, one eye already swollen shut, the other barely open.

An uppercut knocked him from the chair and onto the floor, his face reflected in the shine of the tile, unrecognizable, alien, a bloody pulp of meat barely human anymore.

A heavy boot slammed into his back and he screamed in agony.

Then fear as he lost all feeling below the waist, a sensation he was terrifyingly familiar with.

He's paralyzed me again!

He sobbed uncontrollably at the horror, at the prayers echoing in his head not for the beating to stop, but for his life to end.

For he wanted it to end.

He couldn't go through being wheelchair bound again.

He squeezed his eyes shut, picturing everything he had put his wife through before his miraculous recovery, the brave face she had put on, the sacrifices she had pretended to ignore.

I can't put her through that again. She's better off without me.

Then his little girl filled his vision and he pictured her pointing at his toe, bouncing to the music, the first sign of life below the waist after being shot twice in the back.

And a jolt of pain surged through his body from head to toe.

Thank you, God!

It was the hint of hope he needed to snap out of the self-pity that threatened to take control.

He had to survive for his girls.

And that meant he had to betray his friends.

"Why are they going to Mongolia?"

His sobs renewed. Not for himself, but for the fact he was finally going to talk, he was finally going to give in to the pain and tell the man everything he wanted to know.

He was killing his friends.

"Be-because a former student texted them he was in trouble."

"When did they leave?"

"Last night."

"What flight?"

"I-I don't know. They have a private jet."

"Bullshit." There was a pause. "So, she *is* rich."

"Yes. From her brother." He gasped, another jolt of pain blinding him momentarily, a white hot dagger slicing through his back, his heart hammering from the strain and the terror of what might be to come.

"What's the name of the airline?"

But he couldn't answer, his entire body tense from the agony.

He gasped from another kick to his back.

"Please! Not my back!"

The man stepped around him, staring down at his blood and tear-stained face. "Your back? Why not?"

Milton's heart nearly stopped as he realized he had just made a terrible mistake. He had given his captor a critical piece of information that the man could now capitalize on.

Another kick, this time to the stomach, a love tap compared to the previous, was delivered. "What about your back?"

"N-nothing. It just hurts."

The man pursed his lips then pulled out his phone, tapping away for a moment before a smile slowly crept up one side of his face. "Interesting. You were shot in the back twice, paralyzed for a while, then made a miraculous recovery." The man stared down at him as he shoved his phone back in his pocket. "A miracle man."

Milton said nothing.

His captor grabbed his wallet from the kitchen counter, Milton's pockets emptied before the assault had begun. The man flipped through the photos he kept there. He held up a photo of Sandra. "You're married to a *kaffir*?"

57

Rage gripped Milton at the racist term. "She was born in Trinidad." His eyes narrowed. "Are you South African?"

The man ignored his question. "She's very pretty." He held up a photo of Niskha. "And your daughter. What is she here? Seven? Eight?"

Milton bit his tongue, terrified of where this was going.

"They're both very beautiful." He tossed the wallet back on the counter. "Perhaps I should pay them a visit when I'm done here."

Milton glared at him, helpless to do anything as terror gripped him. "If you lay a finger on them, you'll die a slow, painful death, I swear it!"

The man tossed his head back, laughing. "Oh, I'm shaking. Are you, the cripple, going to kill me?"

Milton summoned all the strength he could muster as he focused his rage on the man towering over him. "If not me, then someone else. I have friends."

"Oh, *you* have friends. Who?"

Milton sneered at him. "You'll find out when they kill you."

Another laugh. "Now I have to know who these friends are, so I know who to keep an eye out for." He eyed him. "I wonder just how much your back can take before you're paralyzed again." He stepped forward and shoved a boot under Milton, flipping him onto his stomach. "Let's find out, shall we?" He raised his boot and dropped it hard.

And thankfully, Milton passed out from the pain, but not before his legs went numb, and he lost all hope.

Approaching Acton/Palmer Residence

St. Paul, Maryland

Lee Fang, exiled Chinese Special Forces, grabbed one of the Glocks in CIA Agent Sherrie White's go bag and slapped a mag in it before handing it forward. Sherrie took it and stuffed it in her belt then held out a freshly manicured hand.

"So sad. I almost never get my nails done, but today, the *one* day I get a chance, the *one* day where I think they might last for more than a weekend, Acton and his wife end up messing things up again."

Fang loaded a second Glock for herself then held out one of her own hands, admiring the bright red she had chosen. "They did a nice job, though."

Sherrie grunted. "For the price, they better."

Fang shrugged as she executed a gymnastic maneuver that had her impressively in the passenger seat a moment later. "Well, you don't want to go to those cheap places. I've seen some pretty horrifying things on

Instagram where people have caught infections because the equipment hasn't been sterilized properly." She held up three magazines for Sherrie to see, then stuffed it into the agent's purse. "Have you seen those fish that eat the dead skin off your feet?"

Sherrie nodded as she took a corner hard. "Yeah, I've always been curious to try it."

"I've done it a few times back in China, but never again. If you think 'manicures gone bad' videos are nasty, you should see the fish ones."

Sherrie's phone rang, attached to the car's Bluetooth. She answered.

"Hello?"

"Status?"

Sherrie winked at Fang, both recognizing Chris Leroux's voice. "Is that any way to greet the love of your life?"

"Sorry. Hi, darling, how's your day?"

"Oh, it was great until my slave-driving boyfriend called and asked if I could go save the world on my day off."

"Yeah, I hear he's a real bastard. You should trade him in for someone else."

Sherrie executed another hairpin turn. "I've considered it, but nobody rocks my world in the sack like he does."

Leroux's throat cleared. "Umm, you're on speaker in the ops center."

Sherrie roared with laughter. "Hi everyone!"

A round of responses had Fang giggling and she was certain the shy Leroux cringing.

"Now that we've got our sex life on public record, anything new?"

"Negative. We've got no further cellphone activity from the house except for some brief Internet access over a cell connection. It looks like someone Googled Dean Milton, so I guess he wanted to know who he has." There was a pause. "I'm concerned he's being tortured. The article the person read was from the University's paper about his recovery."

Sherrie became all business, any trace of the earlier frivolity gone. "You don't think…"

"If they want information, I can't think of a better way to get it."

Sherrie pressed on the accelerator a little harder. "We'll be there in five minutes. ROEs?"

"You're both unsanctioned. Capturing the guy alive with no shots fired would be the ideal."

Fang exchanged a glance with Sherrie. "And if he has other plans?"

"Do what you need to do. We'll clean up the mess later."

Fang reached into the back seat and retrieved two suppressors from the bag. She held them up, giving Sherrie an inquisitive look.

She nodded.

If they did fire, the last thing they needed was the neighbors calling the police. And kneecapping a guy was still capturing him alive, so technically not a violation of their Rules of Engagement.

Fang took another look at her nails and sighed. "I really was looking forward to a girls' night out with no broken nails.

Sherrie shrugged. "We can still go out. We'll just have a story to tell."

Leroux cleared his throat. "Umm, ladies, you do know you can't tell anyone about this?"

Sherrie groaned. "Aww, but how else are we going to have hot guys buy us drinks all night?"

There was a pause. "I think we need to have a talk when you get home."

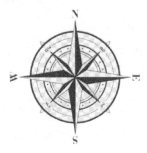

Namjiliin Residence

Ulaanbaatar, Mongolia

Acton checked in both directions, not seeing anything out of the ordinary, then knocked on one of the many doors of the cinderblock rowhouse. A young woman, her eyes red, answered, peering through a sliver of the doorframe, clearly terrified. She said something in Mongolian.

Acton put on his best smile, though he should have ceded his position to Laura. She was better at these things. "Are you Badma Namjiliin?"

She nodded, her eyes widening even more with fear.

"My name is Professor Jim Acton. We spoke on the phone yesterday."

The door yanked open and she flung herself into his arms, sobbing her thanks. Acton held her, then slowly guided her back inside and out of sight of any overly curious neighbors. He extricated himself, handing her off to Laura who took care of the introductions and led her into the home. Acton took one last look out the door before closing it, pausing as something caught his attention.

A vehicle pulling in down the road.

It's just a local.

He pushed the door shut then joined Laura and Badma in the living room, taking a seat across from them. "So, I take it you still haven't heard from him?"

She shook her head, wiping her nose on a handkerchief. "No. Nothing. I've been calling everyone I can think of, but nobody is taking my calls. It's all very strange."

Acton pursed his lips. If calls weren't being taken or returned, it suggested Arban's government employers might be involved. "You said he had a computer?"

She nodded, pointing to a rickety table tucked into the corner of the room. Acton rose, walking over to the computer, shaking his head.

"This looks old."

"It is. It was surplus from the office."

Acton searched for a USB port, finding none. "Uh oh."

Laura joined him. "What?"

"This thing is so old, it doesn't have a USB port."

"Didn't Tommy give you something in case it didn't?"

Acton sighed. "He did. I was just hoping I wouldn't have to use it. Plugging something into a port is one thing. Installing new hardware is something entirely different."

She patted him on the shoulder. "I have faith in you."

Acton set to work, opening up the computer with the toolkit Tommy had provided him, then installing the PCI controller card. It was relatively painless, and within minutes he was up and running. He plugged Tommy's device into the newly installed USB port, connected his phone, then turned to Laura. "I think we're good to go. Give Tommy a shout, let him know we're all set."

Laura dialed then put the call on speaker.

"Hello?"

"It's us. I had to install that USB card. I hope I did it right."

"Is your phone connected?"

"Yes."

"Then give me a minute. I'm dialing now."

Acton's phone rang then went silent, the screen flashing a moment later.

"Good work, Doc. I'm connected. It'll take me a little bit to get past his password, but this is pretty ancient stuff, so shouldn't be too...okay, I'm in."

The door burst open behind them, two men rushing in. Badma screamed as Acton reached for a nearby lamp. He grabbed it and threw it at the nearest man, knocking the gun out of his hand as Laura kicked the couch toward the second, shoving him off balance. Acton surged forward, grabbing the dropped gun off the floor then pistol-whipped his man as Laura leaped onto the couch then across the cushions, snap-kicking hers in the head, knocking him out cold. She collected his weapon, then slapped a hand over the still screaming Badma.

"It's over."

Badma fell silent, nodding, though her entire body still shook.

"Do you know them?"

Badma shook her head. "No."

"Are you okay? What's going on?"

It was Tommy, still on speaker. Acton turned toward Laura's phone, tossed aside in the excitement. "We're okay, Tommy, just give us a minute." He stared at the computer. "But keep working. We might not have much time." He turned to Badma. "Do you have any rope? Something we can tie them up with?"

She stared at him blankly for a moment. "Umm, no, I don't think so."

Acton bent over and yanked the nearest man's belt off, binding his hands as Laura kept a weapon trained on them both. He tied the other up with his belt, then took a blanket from the couch and bound their feet together and to each other.

Tires screeched outside and Laura rushed to the window.

"Four men with guns."

Badma's eyes bulged. "Oh no, what do we do now?"

Laura grabbed her by the arm, heading to the back of the house. "We get the hell out of here."

Stander cursed at the sight of the company car sitting empty. "I told those bastards to wait for backup. They better not have screwed this up."

One of his men, Stefan van Graan, shrugged. "Myburg can handle a couple of professors."

Stander grunted as he drew his weapon. "I'd hope so, but two on three isn't as guaranteed as six on three. We know almost nothing about these professors except that she's rich enough to be able to take a private jet here on a couple of hours' notice. Beyond that, who the hell knows?"

He had people looking into things, but beyond what was publicly known, that they were two well-respected archaeologists, he was American, she was British, and both had been involved in a couple of international incidents as innocent bystanders, they were black boxes.

Nicholas Myburg and his partner had been assigned airport watch the moment they had found out from Du Toit that the professors were heading here. Fortunately, they had found out just in time, and Myburg had spotted the professors the moment they arrived. They had tracked them to their hotel, then here, where they were supposed to wait for reinforcements.

Myburg has always been a bit of a hothead.

If he screwed this up, he'd be off the team. Permanently. If he cost him their payday, he'd be off this earth. Permanently.

Van Graan readied his weapon as they approached the doorway of Arban's house. "Has Du Toit found out anything?"

Stander shook his head. "His last update indicated the Milton guy was spilling everything, but he doesn't know much. We'll use him as leverage over the professors. If they're friends like he says, they'll give us the names of everyone they've spoken to."

"And then?"

"We eliminate them all. The client doesn't want there to be any chance word spreads."

"Harsh."

Stander shrugged. "Big money." He frowned at the shattered door jamb. "Remember, no shooting. We need them alive."

"And if they shoot back?"

"Kneecaps. Always the kneecaps."

Van Graan cocked an ear. "Sounds quiet. Myburg must have them."

Stander pushed open the door and stepped inside the humble home, no better or worse than the strip of residences that lay to either side, the worn plaster chipped away by years of neglect and harsh winters.

Then cursed at what he saw.

Acton grabbed his cellphone, still plugged into Tommy's device, and hid it behind the machine. "Tommy, keep doing what you're doing. We're leaving here. Now. I'm turning the monitor off." He pressed the button then headed for the backdoor and into the alleyway behind the block of rowhouses where Laura was waiting with Badma.

"Do you have a friend you can stay with nearby?"

Badma pointed to their right. "That way."

Laura grabbed her by the arm and herded the trembling woman toward their possible refuge as Acton brought up the rear, his weapon held tight to his side to minimize the chance of a neighbor seeing it.

Badma eased up on their sprint half a dozen units down, then gently knocked on a door. It opened a moment later, a young woman answering, a baby held in each arm. A rapid conversation took place in Mongolian as the suspicious woman eyed the two Westerners.

Acton was about to insist with the gun and sort it out later, when the woman stepped aside, beckoning them to enter. They rushed in and

Acton peered down the alleyway then jerked back, cursing as he prayed the man who had just stepped out from Badma's back entrance hadn't spotted him. He gently shut then locked the door.

"Badma, I want you to stay here until you hear from us. Do you have a phone?"

She shook her head then turned to their hostess, asking something. The woman pointed to the wall, a landline installed. Laura pulled out her phone and stepped over to the ancient device, entering the number written on it into her contacts list.

"Got it."

Acton turned to Badma. "Stay here, out of sight. Make sure your friend knows not to tell anyone you're here."

Laura jotted her number down on a notepad by the phone, tearing off the sheet and handing it to Badma. "If you need to reach us, this is my number. If you think you won't be safe here, go to the Kempinski Hotel Khan Palace and ask for Thomas Granger's room. Can you remember that name? I don't want to write it down. Thomas Granger."

Badma nodded. "Thomas Granger. Yes, I think I can remember."

"Good."

Somebody hammered on the rear door and Badma nearly cried out, thankfully slapping two hands over her mouth as Acton led her to the front room. Their hostess put the two kids on the floor and checked to make sure everyone was out of sight before opening the door.

"Sorry to bother—"

Their hostess tore into the man, screaming at him in Mongolian, a language their pursuer evidently had no knowledge of. The tirade

69

continued for a good minute before the door slammed shut. She stepped into the living area, a smile on her face. "He not know what hit him."

Acton chuckled and Badma hugged the woman hard.

Laura was grinning. "I didn't know you spoke English."

The woman stared at her, clearly having no clue what she had just said.

Badma filled them in. "She doesn't. She just knows some phrases from the movies."

Acton peered out the front window then jerked back into the corner as two men came into view. He risked another peek and watched as they jogged past. He repositioned and spotted two others heading the opposite direction.

Suggesting they had no idea where they were hiding.

And it presented an opportunity.

"We have to get to our car."

"Shouldn't we just hole up here? Wait for them to leave?"

Acton shook his head. "No, they know we're on foot, and they could be calling in reinforcements. In the next few minutes, there could be a dozen of them searching for us, and the fact they barged in with guns tells me they don't care about breaking any laws."

Laura frowned. "What did you have in mind?"

"Badma stays here, you and I get to the car and hightail it out of here."

"And if they see us?"

Acton thought for a moment as he peered back down the street, then examined the room.

And smiled.

He stepped over to an open sewing basket, the tools of the trade neatly organized. He grabbed an awl and held it up. "Can I borrow this?"

Badma translated and their hostess nodded.

Acton tossed the car keys to Laura. "You drive."

Stander stopped at the end of the street, his hands on his hips, staring at the empty field in front of him. If the professors had come this way, there was nowhere to hide.

"What do you think?" asked Myburg.

He glared at the imbecile. "I think you should have followed your orders."

Myburg appeared sufficiently contrite. "Sorry, boss, I thought we could handle it." His eyes widened. "You should have seen them. It was like out of a movie. They've definitely had Special Forces training."

Stander grunted. "That's ridiculous. Two professors? You screwed up, and now you're making up excuses." He turned around. "Let's go house to house. They have to be here."

"And if someone calls the cops?"

"What do you think is in those thick brown envelopes we deliver each week to police headquarters? It's 'look the other way' money. What the hell?" He paused, not believing what he was seeing—two figures walking out of a house halfway down the street.

Two Caucasians.

A man and a woman.

And there was no doubt who it was.

He drew his weapon and sprinted silently toward them.

71

Laura unlocked the car and hopped inside, starting the engine immediately as Acton climbed in the passenger seat. She cursed as she checked her rearview mirror, putting the stick shift into first as Acton glanced over his shoulder at the two men racing toward them.

"Let's go!" he urged, rolling down his window.

She popped the clutch and they surged forward before she hit the brakes beside the vehicle that had delivered the two men he was certain had followed them from the airport. He tried to reach the tire through the window but couldn't. He cursed then stepped out and jammed the awl into the rear tire, then jogged forward as Laura eased the car ahead, repeating the action on the front tire, both immediately sagging to the ground. He sprinted ahead, repeating his efforts on the larger SUV that had delivered the four new hostiles, then hopped in the car, Laura hammering on the gas the moment his foot was clear of the hardpacked dirt road, leaving a cloud of dust behind them, obscuring any shot the men might have had.

He pointed ahead, two more rushing out in front of them, their weapons raised.

Laura cursed as she geared down. "Forward or back?"

"Go right through them!"

She floored it, pressing them both against their seats. A shot rang out, piercing the windshield as they both ducked. Acton popped up to take a look and saw both men diving out of the way. He turned in his seat to see them scrambling to their feet, their weapons rising.

"Turn!"

Laura cranked the wheel and they skidded onto another street, safely out of sight. She took two more quick turns, then eased up on the gas. Slightly. Even on a Sunday drive she was heavy on the metal. "Where to now? Tommy and Mai?"

Acton shook his head. "No, I don't want to put them at risk. What I want to know, though, is how they knew how to find us?"

Laura frowned. "They must be the ones who have Arban, which means they have his phone. They must have seen the text."

Acton sighed. "You're right. I'm probably in his contacts, and the rest is easy enough. But how'd they pick us up here? They'd have to have known we were coming in on a private jet, and when. You can't get that from Google."

Laura shrugged. "These guys seem pretty serious. They were packing some expensive hardware."

Acton agreed. "Yeah, and they were all Caucasian." He cursed. "I should have taken their wallets when I had the chance."

"Their friends showed up pretty quick. There wasn't exactly time. I'm guessing mercenaries, though."

"Agreed. And there were six of them. If someone hired that many, with that kind of hardware, with an obvious willingness to break the law, then they must be connected."

"Yes, but what could be so valuable in Mongolia to need that kind of muscle? This is a poor country. Very poor. And you saw how Arban is living. There's no way he's some drug kingpin or smuggler. So, what could he be involved in that has expensive mercenaries after him?"

Acton grunted. "And us."

"Right, and us."

Acton chewed his cheek as they continued to put distance between them and the hired guns. "Well, the fact they're after us I think gives us some hint of what's going on."

"It does?"

"Well, that text contained nothing beyond the fact he was scared that someone wanted to kill him. It didn't reveal anything else. If they were after some *thing*, then there's no reason to think we have it. We were on the wrong continent."

Laura's head bobbed. "You're right. He must *know* something, and they're afraid he told us."

"Right, and they're trying to tie up loose ends."

"But wouldn't they know from the text message we don't know anything?"

Acton shook his head. "No. If they're pros, they're not going to risk that he might have reached out to us in some other way before they captured him."

"Do you think he's alive?"

Acton sighed. "I don't know. They didn't come in there today with guns blazing, so maybe."

Laura tapped the hole in the windshield. "Someone must not have got the memo."

Acton chuckled. "Instinct? I'd shoot too if someone were coming at me. Unless they were in Reading's favorite British sportscar, then I'd just casually wait for the engine to conk out."

Laura rolled her eyes. "Once you grab on to something, you never let it go."

He flashed a toothy grin. "I can always find a way to work in a good jab." He pointed at a gas station. "Let's fill up while we can, then find someplace to park out of sight."

"Oooh!" squealed Laura.

"Mind out of the gutter, missy."

"Awww."

Acton squeezed her leg. "Okay, one quick shag, then we figure out how to escape those hired killers."

She frowned. "Mood killer."

He climbed out as she brought them to a stop. "I'll make up for it when we get back home."

"You better. The only reason I'm with you is for the sex."

He gave her a look. "You too?" He winked then filled the tank as Laura called Tommy. She cursed.

"What?"

"No signal."

"Lovely. If we can't reach out to people, we could be in serious trouble."

"I think this might be too big for us. We should collect the kids and get back on the plane. See if Dylan and the others can find out what's going on."

Acton agreed. "I think you're right. I just pray they can get to Arban in time."

Tangut Empire, Western Xia
August 17, 1227 AD

Princess Khatun tumbled onto her side as the Khan punched her in the head. The pain from the blow overwhelmed her as she lay there, struggling to recover, the moans and cries of her victim soon overtaking the ringing in her ears.

And she smiled at the sight of the most vicious man in history gripping what was left of his manhood, blood pouring freely onto the animal skins, much like what had happened to the poor beasts upon their own slaughter.

"Die you bastard!" she hissed at him as she rose, the dagger still gripped in her hand. "That is for my father and mother, and for my brothers and sisters." She stepped closer as he stared up at her, agony and rage filling his eyes. "And that is for my people."

"Master, what's wrong?"

She spun toward the entrance to the bedchambers to see the foul henchman from earlier in the day, the one who had brought her here to be soiled by his pig of a leader. His eyes widened at the sight.

"Get her!" groaned the Khan.

The man stood, frozen for a moment, then burst into action. "Get the doctor, now!" he shouted at someone on the other side of the curtains, then he raised his voice, issuing the call that would mean her end. "Guards!"

She bolted for the edge of the tent, yanking the material as hard as she could, the stakes on the other side tearing free. She dropped to her knees and scrambled out the other side, but not before a hand gripped her ankle. She yelped, twisting onto her backside and kicking as hard as she could with her free foot. It connected with something, the grunt from the other side of the tent suggesting someone's head.

The grip loosened.

She scrambled backward, crablike, then rolled and leaped to her feet, quickly gaining her bearings in the dark. Tents stretched as far as the eye could see, Khan's army massive. To the west lay her beloved city, still burning, nothing but the temple left standing.

And her heart ached anew.

There was no one to save her.

Everyone she knew, everything she loved, was gone.

Shouts surrounding her grew as the call to arms continued. They would be upon her any moment now, yet the dark could serve her well if she acted without hesitation.

There was only one hope of escape.

The river.

Her bearings true, she sprinted between the tents, ignoring the sounds of the tragedies occurring on the other side of the animal skins as the women of her empire were systematically raped—there was nothing she could do to help them.

She spotted the river ahead as an arrow whipped past her, embedding into the ground far too close for comfort. She glanced over her shoulder to see half a dozen guards in pursuit. Ducking to her right and between another pair of tents, she cut off any shot, but also lost time. She turned left, resuming her direct line for the river, then broke past the row of tents and into the open, leaving nothing to hide behind.

More shouts for her to stop echoed behind her, but she kept running, her decision made.

For there was only one thing left in her power, only one honorable thing left that she could hope to do.

Deny the murderous Khan his prize.

Arrows whipped past her, and she had to think they were trying to scare her into stopping rather than kill her, likely none of her pursuers wanting to hurt their Khan's prize.

And it would be their final mistake.

She reached the edge of the cliff, the river far below.

And didn't break stride.

She sprinted over the edge, the ground above left behind as she closed her eyes and dove like a bird, her arms out to her side, her legs tucked together behind her as the wind rushed along her body, the roar of the river below rapidly growing louder.

And she said one final prayer, beseeching the spirits to let her join her family, and her people, in the next life.

Unknown Location, Mongolia

Present Day

Arban flinched as he woke to footsteps approaching. His entire body ached from the beating he had received after he had first been caught, the subsequent brief beatings merely to remind him of his situation.

And what that was, he wasn't certain, though he assumed he was going to die.

The door opened, the trailer he had been held in since his return filling with the sounds of heavy equipment operating outside. His eyes immediately went to the man's fists to see if he wore gloves. Instead, he found a bottle of water in one hand, a plastic-wrapped sandwich in the other. Both were tossed on the floor in front of him.

"Eat. I'll be back in a bit to take you to the bathroom."

Arban said nothing, grateful that it was a feeding rather than another beating, and waited for the man to leave. The moment the door shut, he grabbed for the bottle of water and twisted off the cap, gulping down half of it before tearing into the sandwich. He was starving and thirsty, and wasn't sure which was worse. Despite being from a poor country, he had never really been hungry. His brief stay in the United States had been an eyeopener into true decadence, and it had been shocking. Upon his return home, a part of him had regretted the experience.

He had never had anything to compare his simple life to until he left his country. It had taken him until only recently to push that year deep enough to not constantly be regretting what he didn't have here.

For what did he really need to be happy?

He had a beautiful wife, he had a great job that paid decently for his age and station, and now that he had that steady income, they were planning on starting a family to fill their humble yet happy home.

Yeah, what a great job.

He sighed as he finished his sandwich, savoring the last chew before swallowing it and signaling the end of what might be his last meal. It was his job that had gotten him here.

Or was it just his boss?

He couldn't be sure how high the problem went, which was why he didn't know who he could trust. And that was why he had reached out to Acton, the one foreigner he knew whom he happened to have in his phone's contact list, the one foreigner he knew was a good man that would do the best he could to help. Professor Acton had shown him nothing but respect and a genuine interest in his well-being during his year in the United States, making sure to include him in all functions, introducing him to students he thought might be good fits for friendships, and helping him with his studies.

81

He was a good teacher, but also a good friend, despite the age gap.

And he had fueled his interest in archaeology, something there wasn't much funding for here in Mongolia, which was why he had been so excited to get the position he now held—assistant to the Director of Archaeological Preservation. He'd been there barely six months, yet had learned so much already.

Though apparently not when to look the other way.

He sighed as he sipped the last of his water, then closed his eyes, picturing his beautiful wife Badma.

I'm sorry, my love.

He prayed Acton had received his message and was taking action, though what that could be, he had no idea. He had never been given a chance to follow up his lone text message with more details. Acton wouldn't know where to even begin.

And if Acton couldn't help, he was doomed. He couldn't trust anybody, especially the authorities or anyone at the Ministry. There was so much money involved, everyone was probably paid off. Certainly, his boss was. As soon as they had confirmed the exploratory core sample had discovered something that shouldn't have been there, he knew something was wrong.

And it wasn't with the sample.

It was with how everyone reacted, including his boss. A whispered conversation had taken place, and as soon as he saw one of the security men put his hand on his holstered pistol, he knew he was about to die.

Fortunately, he was near the door and had the keys, his boss preferring to be driven around rather than doing the driving himself. It had saved his life. He had managed to reach the city through a stroke of luck. The operation's helicopter was being serviced. He found a signal and executed his plan, the entire drive spent figuring out who to call. Then, with the realization a text was more likely to get through, who to message.

And as he had run down the possibilities, he quickly came to the conclusion that it could be no one in Mongolia. And outside of Mongolia, he knew few people, and even fewer that had a number stored in his phone. And as he scrolled through the names, stumbling upon 'Acton, James,' he realized he was the perfect person to reach out to. For he was the nicest, most caring person he had ever met, and he was certain he would know the right people to call for help.

The fact they hadn't killed him when they captured him meant they were concerned he had told someone of the discovery. The rules were clear, the agreement in writing. If anything of historical importance was found on the site, all operations would have to halt immediately so the discovery could be examined, and should it prove to be of significance, the entire project could be canceled.

Costing the foreign owners billions in lost profits, not to mention the loss of the tens of millions already invested, the diversion of a river only one of the massive undertakings involved in getting the project going. This project was too big to be allowed to fail. He realized that now. His inexperience, his naiveté, had led him to believe he and the others from the Ministry were serving some noble purpose, but in reality, they were window dressing, only there for show, to give a rubber stamp at the end of the day, no matter what might have been found.

He had been a fool.

Yet what choice had he had? It was his job, he had been assigned to the team, and he guessed that nobody had ever expected to find anything. After all, they were in the middle of nowhere, and there had never been any records of even a village being located here in the past. What they had found, by chance, shouldn't be there, and the archaeologist in him had him wondering what it could be. Handcrafted wood and a skeletal hand had been found in the core sample at a depth of about thirty feet.

It could be anything, or it could be nothing.

Yet by law, it had to be investigated, and by law, historical finds always took precedence over any development, no matter how valuable. Which was why, he now realized, these big projects always went through—the outcome was predetermined through corruption and graft.

They had interrogated him for hours, demanding to know who he had texted, who the professor was and why he had chosen him, who else he had told. He had resisted at first, but soon the pain was too much, and he had told them everything.

Almost everything.

For there was one bit of hope still remaining that might save him, and save whatever it was they had discovered.

Ulaanbaatar, Mongolia

"I give up. It's just no use."

Laura leaned her head back against the headrest in frustration. She had tried to reach their travel agent several dozen times but either the call wouldn't go through or it would be dropped within seconds. It was quite evident that international cellphone service in Mongolia was garbage compared to what they were used to.

James pointed at a shop up ahead, an old woman sitting out front, a sign in several languages, the English reading 'Phone Booth.' Her eyes narrowed. *"That's* a phone booth?"

James shrugged. "In Mongolia, I guess a table with a phone on it is a phone booth. Worth a try."

She sighed. "I'm willing to try anything right about now."

She brought the car to a halt and climbed out, walking over to the woman. "Do you speak English?"

The woman tapped the sandwich board, a price in Mongolian currency shown for international calls. Not having had time to get any local currency, she handed over twenty dollars.

"Is this enough?"

The woman's eyes widened, a toothless smile spreading. She tapped an old phone, a line running from it into the store behind her. Laura knelt and lifted the receiver, pressing it to her ear, then dialed their agent's number.

She sighed with relief when Mary picked up on the second ring.

"Hello?"

"Hi, Mary, it's Laura. No time for a chinwag. We need to get out of Mongolia fast. Can you have the jet prepared and waiting for us? We're going to collect Tommy and Mai then head straight for the airport."

"Oh, thank God! I've been trying to reach you for almost an hour!"

"Why, what's wrong?"

"Your plane is gone."

"What?" Laura's chest tightened and she became lightheaded for a moment. She turned and beckoned James to join her. He was soon out of the car and at her side. "What do you mean the plane is gone?"

His eyebrows shot up.

"I mean the Mongolian government revoked the landing permit and ordered the company to fly it out immediately."

"That's incredible! Why would they do that?"

"I have no idea. It happened so quickly. I found out about it myself after the plane had already left."

Laura squeezed her forehead with her free hand. "Wait. Does that mean Tommy and Mai are on it?"

"I'm not sure. I would think so. After all, they were staying at the same hotel as the pilot and copilot, so you'd think they'd all have left together."

Laura sighed with relief. If the kids were safe, that was the most important thing. But now they'd have to figure out another way to leave. "Can you arrange another charter?"

"Maybe, but not from your regular lease-share. They won't touch it with a ten-foot pole now. Do you want me to arrange a commercial flight?"

Laura nodded. "Yes, do that, but we need to confirm that Tommy and Mai are safely out of the country."

"I'll try to find out for you. What number can I reach you at?"

"I have no idea. We've lost James' phone. I still have mine, but reception is terrible. We can't go to the hotel, because they could be waiting for us there."

"Who?" She could hear the concern in Mary's voice.

"We don't know, but some men just tried to either kill us or kidnap us, I'm not sure."

"Oh no! What is it with you two?"

Laura grunted. "No idea. Listen, book all four of us on a few flights spread out over the next few days, say every twelve hours, and try texting us the info. Text Tommy and Mai too. A text is more likely to get through than a call. We'll try to make at least one of them."

"I will. And Laura?"

87

"Yes?"

"Be careful."

Laura gave a pathetic laugh. "We always try."

She ended the call and handed the receiver back to the old lady who smiled again, the twenty dollars still clutched in her hand. Laura climbed back in the car along with James, and they pulled from the curb.

He looked at her. "I've got a million questions."

She sighed. "And I've got a million answers you're not going to like."

Kempinski Hotel Khan Palace

Ulaanbaatar, Mongolia

Tommy watched helplessly as Mai's desperate calls to Laura's phone continued unanswered, the cellphone service here horrendous. All they could do was hope the professors were fine, and operating under that assumption, that meant he still had a job to do.

Analyze the data.

He began running through the standard documents directories, using his custom translation app playfully nicknamed by Acton as Tommy's Text Translator, the Mongolian documents proving painfully boring.

"Can I help?"

He shrugged. "Can you read Mongolian?"

She gave him a look. "That's not helpful."

He sighed. "You're right. I'm sorry, I'm just worried about them. I just wish there was something we could do."

She jabbed a finger at his laptop. "Find something that can help. The quicker we find something, the quicker we can get out of this godforsaken country."

He shook his head. "There's just so much. This is going to take forever. He's got stuff going back years here."

She stopped her pacing. "Just narrow it down to anything from the last month. Can you do that?"

He smiled. "My girlfriend, the genius." He immediately re-filtered the search results, cutting down the list considerably. "That's better!"

There was a knock at the door that had both their hearts pounding, and he found he was holding his breath in case whoever it was might hear him.

"Should I answer it?" whispered Mai, answering her own question by retreating from the door.

He wasn't sure. "It might be them. Or maybe our food." He pointed at the door. "Look."

Her eyes bulged and she shook her head. "*You* look!"

He rolled off the bed and tiptoed to the door, peeking through the peephole.

And sighed with relief.

"It's that stewardess. I think she's drunk."

Clarice pounded on the door. "I know you're in there! What are you two doing? Having"—hiccup—"sex? Can I join you?" A heaving sound erupted. "Men are pigs. Especially pilots. Especially *co*pilots!" Another hiccup. "Can you believe they left me when I went to the bathroom?" A manly burp vented. "I'm going to fall down now." There was a loud noise.

"What should we do?"

Mai shrugged. "We can't leave her out there."

He sighed then opened the door. Clarice was passed out on the floor, as advertised. Her keycard was gripped in her hand, a bottle of something local in the other. He pried the card loose, handing it to Mai, then picked the passed out woman up off the floor, draping her arm over his shoulders as he half carried, half dragged her to her room. Mai opened the door and they both got her onto the bed then performed the Bacchus Maneuver to position her on her side in case she vomited. Mai dumped the bottle's potent brew down the bathroom sink, then placed the keycard on the nightstand before they both beat a hasty retreat back to their room, only to find Tommy's phone ringing.

He dove for it but it went to voicemail before he could answer. Cursing, he waited, the phone finally vibrating in his hand with a message. He dialed in and put it on speaker.

"Hi guys, it's Laura. There's a problem. It looks like the government ordered our plane to leave. We don't know what's going on. I'm hoping the fact you're not answering means they already told you, and you left as part of the crew. We'll try to find our own way out of the country, but before we do, we need to know that you've actually left. Call me as soon as you've got this message. If you can't reach me, call my travel agent. I left you the number. Tell her your status. We won't be leaving without her help, so she'll get the message to us. Good luck. Love you guys."

Acton/Palmer Residence

St. Paul, Maryland

Sherrie pulled the car into Acton's driveway and headed for the front door as Fang sprinted to the backyard. Fang heard shouts from inside as Sherrie confronted an obvious intruder. Fang tried the sliding back door to find it locked, so grabbed the handle and jerked the entire door up and out of its frame, tossing it aside as she surged into the kitchen. Sherrie was at her eleven o'clock, with the hostile at her nine, his weapon aimed at Sherrie, Milton held against him as a human shield.

Fang took aim and shot the man in the hand, his weapon dropping to the floor followed by Milton a moment later as the assailant cried out in agony, gripping his hand with its new piercing. Sherrie rushed forward as Fang covered her, quickly binding the man's hands and feet together before patting him down, tossing anything of interest on the kitchen counter.

Fang took a knee beside the badly beaten Milton, shaking her head at what had been done to the poor man. "Where does it hurt?"

"Everywhere." He gasped. "But my back. I think he might have broken my back."

Fang quickly checked him head to toe, finding some possibly cracked ribs and no sensation below the waist. She gave Sherrie a glance, subtly shaking her head. "Just stay still, try not to move."

Milton nodded then lunged forward, grabbing her weapon from her belt, aiming it at their prisoner.

"What are you doing?" cried Fang, standing back.

"He-he threatened to rape Sandra and Niskha."

Fang assumed he was referring to his wife and daughter. She took as gentle a tone as she could. "Listen, we need him alive. He has information."

"I don't care. He needs to die."

The assailant glared at Milton wide-eyed. "Kill me! Pull the trigger. If you don't, I'm going to pay a visit to those tasty treats. Remember, I know where those little kaffirs live now!"

Milton's hand trembled, the weapon shaking uncontrollably as tears rushed down his cheeks, the pain and anger mixing into a potent brew that threatened to explode.

Fang knelt beside him again. "Greg, we need him. He's just trying to bait you." She tried another tact. "Listen, if you want him dead, then when this is all done, I'll take care of it. But don't you do it."

He looked at her through swollen eyes, his face unrecognizable, the only reason she knew it was him was because she had been told he was here. "I want to," he whispered.

She stared at him, understanding his rage, understanding his desire. She had been there before. And had pulled that trigger. "Have you ever killed before?"

He shook his head. "No."

"Do you plan on doing it again?"

His eyes darted to her before returning to his target. "I-I hope not."

"Then don't do it. Killing one person, in the heat of the moment, is something you'll never forgive yourself for, unless you're going to make a habit of it." She put a hand on his shoulder, gently squeezing. "Your daughter wouldn't want her father to become a murderer for her. They're safe now. He's finished."

The arm holding the gun dropped to the floor and Milton fell backward, exhausted, his hand loosening its grip. Fang retrieved the weapon and tucked it back in her belt as Sherrie approached, having watched the proceedings quietly nearby.

"An ambulance is on the way." Sherrie grabbed a cloth shopping bag hanging from a hook in the kitchen then stuffed their prisoner's personal items inside. She cut the ties binding his feet then hauled him up off the floor. "You're coming with us. Any sudden movement, any attempt to escape, I shoot you in the knees then start picking body parts to remove while you watch naked in a mirror." She kneed him in the nuts and the man grunted. "Starting with those." She led him away, her gun pressed against his back while Fang waited with Milton.

"You've gotta warn Jim and Laura. These people are after them."

"Who are they?"

"I have no idea, but he has an accent. I think South African."

Fang pursed her lips. "Interesting. We know he was talking to someone in Mongolia. We're trying to track down who. They're definitely horny to find the professors. Any idea why?"

Milton shook his head and winced. "Wait. Do you know about the text message?"

"Yes. Do you know what it's all about?"

"N-no. S-sorry."

"Don't worry about it. "Fang reached out and put a hand on his shoulder. "Stay still. If there's any damage to your spine, we want to minimize it."

Tears escaped Milton's eyes and he squeezed them shut, clearly trying to stop himself from sobbing.

"It's going to be okay." A siren in the distance grew close. "They're almost here, then they'll take good care of you. Langley will make sure you have protection assigned to you, probably local." She squeezed his shoulder. "Listen, I have to leave here when they get here, okay?"

Milton nodded. "That's—that's fine. I know you can't risk being mixed up in anything like this." He reached up and took her hand. "Thank you for saving me."

She flashed him a smile, squeezing his hand. "Thanks for making an otherwise dull day interesting."

He grunted. "Any time?"

She resisted the urge to laugh so as not to trigger his own, instead gently placing his hand down by his side as the front door opening signaled her departure.

And as she headed out the back door, she vowed that if Milton never walked again, neither would their prisoner.

Operations Center 3, CIA Headquarters

Langley, Virginia

"This is interesting."

Leroux turned to Randy Child. "What?"

"The professors' plane has taken off."

Leroux's eyes narrowed. "What?"

"Yeah. About an hour ago."

Leroux rose and walked over to Child's station to check the intel. "But that doesn't make any sense. They've only been there a few hours."

Sonya Tong turned to face them. "Maybe they found who they were looking for."

Child shrugged. "No idea, but the plane is out of Mongolian airspace and according to their flight plan, is heading for South Korea."

Leroux returned to his station. "South Korea? Why would they go there and not come home?"

Another shrug. "Vacation?"

Leroux sighed. "Anything's possible with them." He slapped his hands on his knees. "Well, I guess we can stand down, then." He leaned back in his chair. "I love it when these things turn out to be nothing."

Tong agreed. "Me too."

"Let's let Dylan know. I'm sure he's worried."

"Will do, but he's on radio silence according to the system. He won't get the message for at least a few hours."

"Better late than never." Leroux's stomach growled and he patted it. "I'm heading to the cafeteria. I'm starved. Team A, you guys take an hour then relieve Team B. Who knows when we'll get another chance for a break." Leroux headed for the door and Child cleared his throat.

"Umm, sir?"

Leroux sighed, knowing it wasn't going to be good news. "What?"

"Umm, well, I've got another Echelon intercept that you're going to want to see."

"Between who?"

"Laura Palmer and her travel agent."

Leroux's shoulders sagged. "Let me guess. It happened *after* the plane left."

"Yes."

"And it wasn't from in the air."

"No, a landline in Mongolia."

Leroux cursed. "I should have known." He pointed at Tong. "Have lunch brought in. I have a feeling this is going to be a long day."

Acton/Palmer Residence

St. Paul, Maryland

Fang climbed into the back seat with their prisoner. Sherrie, having moved the car onto the street while Fang awaited the ambulance, pulled from the curb as the first police car turned the corner. She steered to the side to let him by, then continued as if they were merely locals heading out for some shopping.

Fang aimed her weapon at their prisoner. "You better pray he's okay, or I promise you either a very short life, or a very long one you won't want to live."

He eyed her, showing no evidence of fear. "What is it with you two?"

Sherrie looked in the rearview mirror. "We don't like it when people mess with our friends."

"So, he's a friend of yours?"

"Consider him our best friend, so choose your words carefully. Who do you work for?"

"Nobody."

Fang hammered the top of his wounded hand with the butt of her Glock and he cried out, blood surging from under the gauze wrapped around it, an open emergency kit on the floor, Sherrie evidently carrying out some first aid as she waited for Fang to join them. "Why were you there?"

"Got the wrong house."

Another rap, another cry, the hand already showing signs of additional trauma.

"The next one's going to really hurt," warned Fang. "Why the interest in Professor Acton?"

"He's an old college buddy?"

Fang dropped the hammer hard and the resulting roar was deafening, the bones of the hand shattered. "I've got all day."

"So do I," gasped the man, wincing.

She raised her weapon again and he held up his good hand. "Please, no more."

"Tell us what you know." She motioned toward Sherrie. "The truth, or I let her take you apart, piece by piece."

"Fine, but I don't know much. I got a phone call from an old buddy who asked me to find this Professor Acton and find out what he knew about something in Mongolia. That's all I know."

"Bullshit."

"I swear, that's it."

"And what was this thing in Mongolia?"

"I have no clue. He didn't tell me. I didn't need to know until I had Acton, and since I never got him, he never told me."

Fang suppressed her frown. Unfortunately, that part of the story did make sense. "What's your name?"

"Bill Shephard. William."

Fang grabbed his wallet from the bag of his belongings, finding nothing but several hundred dollars in cash. "Do you always go out without ID?"

"When I'm doing something illegal, yes."

"No fakes?"

"There's no law that says I have to carry ID."

Sherrie glanced in the rearview mirror. "Unless you're driving a car. Did you walk?"

He shrugged, wincing as the action moved his shattered hand. "I took a chance."

Sherrie reached into her purse then activated an app on her CIA issue phone, handing it back to Fang. "Take his photograph and fingerprints, then upload it. We'll know who he is soon enough."

Fang complied, making sure to use the broken hand, then tapped the button to send the data to Leroux's team. The phone rang a few moments later and she answered. "Hello?"

"Fang?"

"Yes."

"It's Chris. We've got an ID on your guy. His name is Willem Du Toit. He's got quite the record. Former South African Special Forces, went legit private military, then dropped off the radar for the most part, though he's been linked to several mercenary groups over the past decade. The South Africans want him. When you're done with him, we'll hand him over to the FBI so they can arrange extradition."

"Okay, we're bringing him in. Should be there shortly." She ended the call, returning Sherrie's phone to her purse, then smiled at her prisoner. "So, Mr. Du Toit, you're a very popular man."

He frowned. "That was quick. Just who the hell do you two work for?"

Fang smiled. "I'm a bored housewife. She's sleeping with the boss." She took his wounded hand and squeezed slightly. "Now, *if* our friend survives unscathed, you'll be going back to South Africa. What's the name of your contact in Mongolia?"

He grunted. "Lady, you're an amateur when it comes to pain where he's concerned."

She squeezed harder and he cried out, his entire body tensing as every vein in his neck was revealed. "It's not that long a drive, but my friend can take the scenic route."

Sherrie glanced back. "Through Michigan!"

Fang eased her grip slightly. "What's his name? You know we're going to find out anyway, and he doesn't need to know how."

He glared at her, his chest heaving as he tried to recover. She squeezed again.

Hard.

Another roar of agony.

"Okay! Okay! That's enough!"

She let go.

"His name is Hendrick Stander. He was my commanding officer back in the day, before we went private. But you don't want to mess with him. He'll kill you as soon as look at you. Your friends are probably already dead if they're planning on interfering. There's just too much at stake."

Fang's eyes narrowed. "What do you mean?"

He shook his head vehemently. "No, that's all I'm saying. I don't care what you do to me. He'll have me killed in prison. He's too well-connected."

Fang sat back, regarding the man. She believed him. There'd be nothing else coming out of his mouth, but now they had a name.

It wasn't much, but it was a start.

Kempinski Hotel Khan Palace

Ulaanbaatar, Mongolia

"I don't know how you can be working at a time like this! We're stranded in Mongolia, and there are bad guys after us!"

Tommy kept working, trying to ignore Mai's pacing. "What would you have me do?"

"I don't know! Show me that you're at least concerned?"

"Of course I am, but there's nothing we can do about it." He sighed, tearing his attention away from the photos he had discovered in Arban's email. "Look, you know the professors aren't going to leave us here. Nobody knows we're here except for them. They'll find some way to get us out of here, but until then, we should try to remain calm, and be ready to leave on a moment's notice." He paused, thinking of something she could do to occupy her time. "Are you all packed?"

She pointed at their carry-ons by the door. "Within about two minutes of hearing that message."

He stared at her for a moment. "Wanna have sex? That'll take your mind off things."

She glared at him.

He chuckled. "I was just joking."

"No, you weren't."

He grinned. "You're right, I wasn't." He beckoned her over, pointing at the screen. "What does that look like to you?"

She climbed onto the bed and peered at the image, one of several dozen he had found in Arban's email, stored locally on his computer. "A hand?"

"That's what I was thinking. And it's just bones, so it's old, right?"

She nodded, Mai the archaeologist of the pair. "What are these photos of?"

He shrugged, zooming the photo out, revealing a long table with what appeared to be tubes of rock laid out in sections, one part revealing something entirely different for half a dozen feet. "It's kind of weird. What does that look like to you?"

She pursed her lips for a moment, their predicament evidently forgotten. Her eyes widened. "Core samples!"

"Huh?"

"Core samples. They essentially drill these long hollow pipes into the ground, then they pull it all out and open them up. It allows them to see what's under the ground for as deep as they want to go. Scientists do this all the time. These look like the types of samples they would take at a mine site to see what minerals are underneath." She pointed at the void.

"It looks like they found something other than rock or sand at this point."

"Well, all the photos on Arban's computer were of this section at various angles. From the metadata attached to the phone, and the timestamps of the emails, I think he took the photos, immediately emailed them to himself, then several hours later, sent that text message to the Doc."

Her eyes narrowed. "Then what happened during all that time?"

"Whatever it was, it couldn't have been good." He tapped the screen. "And it probably had something to do with this." He turned to Mai. "What would normally happen in a situation like this?"

"What do you mean?"

"I mean, you're at a mine site, taking core samples, and you find some old dude's hand mixed in with your rocks. What would happen?"

She tapped her chin several times. "I don't know about Mongolia, but in a lot of places, drilling would stop until the find could be investigated. If it turned out to be nothing, or something that could easily be moved safely, then drilling would continue after that was completed. If it turned out to be significant, it could stop the project entirely."

Tommy chewed his cheek. "Sounds like something someone wouldn't want to risk."

She stared at him. "You mean you think this entire thing could be about keeping a mining operation going?"

He shrugged. "You've got a better theory?"

She shook her head. "No. It's just kind of terrifying to think people might kill over something like that."

Tommy jutted his chin toward the window. "Take a look outside. We're not exactly in Kansas anymore."

Her eyes narrowed. "Kansas? We live in Maryland."

He chuckled. "Never mind."

A knock at the door silenced them both. Mai stared at him, her eyes wide with terror. He rolled off the bed as stealthily as he could then tiptoed toward the door and peered through the peephole.

And sighed in relief, unlocking the door and opening it. Acton and Laura entered silently, and Tommy locked the door behind them as Mai leaped from the bed and into Laura's arms.

"I knew you wouldn't leave us!"

Laura hugged her, kissing the top of her head as Acton gave Tommy a more manly greeting. "Of course not. But what are you doing here? Didn't they call you when the plane was ordered out of the country?"

Mai shook her head. "Nobody called."

"You never left your room?"

She shook her head again. "Not for a second."

Tommy cleared his throat. "That's not actually true. We did leave for maybe five minutes."

Acton frowned. "Why? We told you explicitly *not* to leave the room under any circumstances."

Tommy's stomach flipped as if he had been chastised by his father. "It wasn't our fault. It was that idiot flight attendant. She got drunk and started hammering on our door, then passed out in the hallway. We couldn't leave her there."

Mai agreed. "We took her to her room and made sure she was okay, then came back." Her eyes widened. "Do you think they could have called us while we were doing that?"

Acton shook his head. "Who knows? You'd think they'd try more than once. I have a feeling the pilots were collected and taken to the airport. They wanted that plane gone and didn't care about the rest of the flight crew."

"But why would they do that?"

"To trap us here."

"But why?"

Acton shrugged. "Haven't the foggiest." He nodded toward Tommy's laptop on the bed. "Any luck?"

Tommy grunted. "Now that you mention it, we did find something interesting, but aren't quite sure what to make of it." He grabbed the laptop and placed it on the table in the corner. The two professors sat, flipping through the images.

Laura pointed at one. "Core samples. Looks like from a mine."

"That's what Mai thought."

"Hello! What's this?" Acton zoomed in on the photo Tommy had been examining earlier, revealing the skeletal hand. "Looks like they found something."

Mai scratched her arm. "Something worth killing for?"

Acton shrugged. "If Mongolia has the same type of rules we do, a discovery like this could bring the entire mining operation to a halt, and could even kill the project."

Laura folded her arms. "Funny you should use that word. Whatever is going on, somebody seems willing to kill to make sure this information doesn't get out. Are we sure this is why they targeted Arban?"

Acton leaned back in his chair. "No, but do you have a better idea?"

Laura frowned. "No, I guess not."

Tommy pointed at the image. "And the timestamps support the theory."

Laura looked at him. "What do you mean?"

"These photos were taken and immediately sent to his email. My guess is they have a good Internet connection at the site, probably a satellite uplink, and have a Wi-Fi network set up for the workers. Arban must have used that to transmit the images, then a few hours later, he sent you that text. It's too much of a coincidence to not be related."

Acton sighed, his head bobbing slowly. "I agree. If only we knew where this was taken. We could find out who's behind this, and get that to Dylan. He might be able to have the folks back home apply some pressure on the Mongolian government."

"We do know."

Acton's eyebrows shot up. "Huh?"

"The GPS coordinates are embedded in the images."

"They are?"

"Yeah, most phones are set to automatically record the location of any photo that's taken. When you send the photo or upload it, that metadata is preserved unless you explicitly tell your phone not to."

Acton cursed. "Another reason to hate the Internet."

Tommy shrugged. "I like it. I can park my car anywhere, take a photo, and never worry about not finding it."

Acton eyed him. "Most of us just remember. It's why millions of cars aren't lying around the country abandoned."

Tommy grinned. "If they're all parked nicely, how would you know?"

Acton chuckled. "Okay, I'll give you that one." He pointed at the image. "Can you show us where this was taken?"

Tommy extracted the GPS coordinates and plugged them into mapping software he had already downloaded onto his computer in the event they didn't have a speedy connection. He pointed at a flag on the screen. "We're here, and this image was taken here." He indicated another flag outside of the city in the middle of nowhere. "That looks like it's a couple of hundred miles from here."

Acton agreed. "Yeah, and who knows what the roads are like. It would take at least a few hours. The message was sent about four hours after the email. Maybe he managed to get here before he was captured."

Laura whistled. "That would be one hell of a chase."

Acton pursed his lips as he stared at the map. "It would all depend on the vehicle and the driver. The fact he was caught suggests he never really lost them. They might have been in his rearview mirror the entire time."

"How terrifying!" cried Mai.

"Tell me about it." Acton sat forward. "Okay, we need to get out there and see what there is to see."

Tommy's jaw dropped. "Are you crazy? Isn't that like jumping into the *sarlaac's* pit?"

Acton smiled. "I think Boba Fett survived."

Tommy hissed with excitement. "Wouldn't that be awesome?"

Acton reached for his phone then cursed. "Forgot, it's at Arban's." He gestured at Laura. "Can you upload the coordinates into Laura's phone? The GPS will still work without a cell connection, right?"

Tommy nodded. "Yes. I set up both your phones a while back to have the maps stored locally, so you'll be good to go." Laura handed over the phone and Tommy went to work. He handed it back a few moments later. "You're all set."

Mai put a hand on Tommy's shoulder. "Are we coming with you?"

Laura vehemently shook her head. "Absolutely not. Stay here until you hear from us, or the travel agent. She's supposed to be booking tickets for us on a commercial flight. I want you on the first flight out of here, no questions."

Tommy frowned. "But we can be of help."

"No, this is too dangerous. We never should have brought you in the first place."

Tommy drew a breath, squaring his shoulders. "It was our choice, and if you hadn't, you wouldn't know where to go now."

Acton put his hand over Mai's, still resting on Tommy's shoulder. "You're right, we wouldn't, and we're grateful. But there's nothing else you can do to help us. You've got all the data off his computer, and you've found us a location to start looking for Arban. Get Mai out of the country and to safety, so we don't have to worry about you. Remember, Dylan knows we're here, but he doesn't know you're here. If he arranges something, it's likely going to be fast, and for two."

Tommy sighed. "You're right. Okay, when she calls, we're out of here."

Acton pointed a finger at him. "First flight."

"First flight."

"Good. Now, stay in the room and make sure at least one of you is always within earshot of the phone. Text us when something happens. We'll eventually get the message, I'm sure."

"Okay."

Hugs and handshakes were exchanged, and the two professors left the room, Tommy locking the door behind them. He turned to Mai. "I can't believe we're going to leave them here."

She shook her head. "I don't know about you, but I'm not leaving, not until we know for sure Dylan can save them."

Tommy's eyes shot wide as his heart hammered. "Are you nuts?"

She stared at him. "After everything they've done for me, for us, you can ask me that?"

He sighed. "Then I better get to work."

He grabbed his laptop and hopped back onto the bed. "How the hell do you reach a CIA secret agent?"

She shrugged. "Call M?"

"Wrong country. But it's not the worst idea."

Sinai Hospital

Baltimore, Maryland

Sandra Milton's entire body ached from sobbing, and from standing in a constant vigil from the moment she had arrived, someone she had never met calling to tell her what had happened and where he had been taken. She wasn't sure what was going on, though she had little doubt it was related to their good friends, Jim and Laura.

And at this moment, she'd smack him in the face for getting them involved.

Yet it wasn't their fault. Whoever had done this had come looking for Acton and Laura, which meant they didn't know that they were already in Mongolia. Whoever had done this to her poor husband was here because of the text message that had been sent, so would have come regardless.

And if they hadn't gone, yes, Greg wouldn't have been there to check on the house, but that would have only meant the same would have been done to her friends, including Laura, something she couldn't fathom wishing for.

There was only one person to blame for this.

The person who had done it.

And the phone call she had received from an anonymous woman assured her the man was in custody, and was no longer a threat.

She hoped that meant he would die a slow, painful death for what he had done.

She stepped away from the door as the doctor emerged. "How is he?"

He frowned. "I won't lie to you, Mrs. Milton, he's in bad shape. He's got several cracked ribs, internal bleeding, and significant trauma to his spine. With his history, this is concerning."

She didn't care about that. She would gladly take care of him for the rest of his life. All she cared about was that she be given the opportunity. "Will he live?"

"Barring any complications, yes, I think so."

Her legs wavered and he reached out, catching her as she gasped in relief at the news. He guided her into a seat on the opposite side of the hallway, then knelt in front of her. "We're taking him into surgery now. We should know in a few hours."

She reached into her purse for a package of tissues. "And his back? Will-will he walk?"

The doctor frowned. "I just can't say. He seems to have no feeling below the waist at the moment. It could simply be swelling. Time will tell."

Her shoulders shook and she took a deep breath, holding it, as she struggled to maintain her composure. Her phone rang in her purse and she ignored it. She stared up at the doctor. "I know you'll do your best."

He patted her on the shoulder. "You can count on it." He rose as her husband was pushed out of the room on the gurney. She jumped to her feet and rushed to his side, taking his hand as she walked with him.

"I'm here, honey. You're going to be okay."

He managed a weak smile and squeezed her hand with barely any strength. "Hug Niskha for me."

The mention of their daughter had the tears flowing freely. "I will. We'll both be here when you come out."

He shook his head. "No. Don't let her see me like this. She's too young."

She nodded. "I understand."

A nurse blocked her from continuing. "I'm sorry, ma'am, but you can't come any farther."

The gurney continued and she let go of her husband's hand. "I love you!"

A weak thumbs up was given, and as the doors swung shut, any confidence she had in the hospital staff was forgotten as she collapsed into a ball in the corner, certain she had spoken to her beloved husband for the last time.

And her damned phone rang yet again.

St. Paul's University

St. Paul, Maryland

Rita left another message on Sandra Milton's phone then hung up, not sure what to do. The phone call she had received from one of the university's students sounded like a prank call, but the earnestness in the boy's voice soon had her convinced it was real.

Two students, trapped in Mongolia, their professors, including one who taught at this university whom she knew well, trapped with them.

And apparently, Dean Milton, her boss, was the only person they could think of that might be able to help.

And he wasn't answering, nor was his wife.

There was a rap on the doorframe as Professor Damiani poked his head inside. "Is the Dean in?"

She shook her head. "No. I've been trying to reach him, but he's not answering."

"Well, I thought he should know that something's happened at Jim Acton's place."

Rita's heart leaped into her throat. "What do you mean?"

"There was some sort of home invasion, I guess. Dave Kelley lives on his street and said there were police and an ambulance there earlier. They took someone out on a stretcher. Looked pretty bad. I'm guessing it was Jim. Do you know where Laura is?"

Rita's eyes widened as she processed the information. Acton and Laura were in Mongolia, which meant that whoever had been taken out on a stretcher wasn't one of them. She gasped as she realized who it had to be. "Oh my god!" She grabbed her purse and rushed out the door.

"What?"

"It's not Jim! It's Greg!"

Ulaanbaatar, Mongolia

"You've lost them?"

Stander didn't need to be an expert to tell Conrad was pissed. "For now. They'll show up. There are not a lot of places for them to go. We're watching their hotel and the airport, and our government contacts have put them on a watchlist. They won't be getting out of the country."

"It's a big country."

"Yes, but with almost nobody in it. We'll find them eventually."

"And what about that text message?"

"I'm still waiting to hear from my man in the US. At the moment, there's no evidence it went beyond the professors."

"I've got a file on my desk that says these professors are *very* rich."

"So?"

Conrad growled. "So? People with money who disappear pose questions, questions that demand answers. That little bastard reached out to probably the only people who can actually hurt us."

Stander stared at the decrepit rowhouse Arban called home. "Maybe that's why he chose them."

"I doubt it. These people don't flaunt their wealth from what your background check shows. I think he just got lucky. You're sure that email he sent wasn't forwarded?"

"Yes, but somebody pulled the data off his hard drive. We found a phone and a newly installed USB card hooked up when we searched his house. The phone traced back to Professor Acton."

"And who was dialed into it?"

"A US number. Thomas Granger."

"And he is?"

"A nobody now, but somebody with his name hacked the Department of Defense mainframe as a teenager. I'm guessing with what we found, he's one and the same."

Conrad cursed. "So, that means the email with the pictures Arban took are with a hacker. They could be everywhere now."

Stander shook his head. "I don't think so. We're monitoring the web and haven't seen anything. Besides, I don't think he's in the US."

"What do you mean?"

"I think he's here. He would have needed a very stable connection to pull that much data. There's no way he'd be able to stay connected long enough from overseas."

"Did the professors bring him with them?"

"They must have."

"But I thought the manifest only had two passengers."

"It did. They must have come in commercial."

There was a pause. "Or they smuggled them in somehow."

Stander shook his head. "No way. Security would have caught them."

"Could they have stayed on the plane?"

Stander rolled his eyes at the notion. "No. As soon as that thing powered down it would have turned into a hotbox. No, he's in the city somewhere, probably holed up in a hotel."

"But how?"

Stander's eyes widened and a smile spread as a thought occurred to him. "He came in as crew!"

Operations Center 3, CIA Headquarters
Langley, Virginia

"My God, these guys are clever."

Leroux turned to Tong. "What do you mean?"

"Well, you know how that travel agent's phone call referred to their students Tommy and Mai being there?"

"Yeah. Have you figured it out?"

She pointed at the screen, showing a document listing the flight crew, Thomas Granger and Mai Trinh highlighted. "They had them come in as part of the flight crew."

Leroux shook his head at the audacity. "How the hell did they manage that?"

She shrugged. "Big bucks means you can do pretty much whatever you want."

Leroux agreed. "Must be nice." He folded his arms. "Okay, so they bring them in undercover so to speak, so that means they knew it could be dangerous."

"Which proved true."

Leroux grunted. "It usually does with them." He chewed his cheek, staring at the intel displayed on the screens. "So, where are they now? They should all be in the same hotel, right? I mean the flight crew."

Tong frowned. "We're not exactly talking a state of the art country here. Finding out where they might be staying could take some time."

Leroux shook his head. "To hell with that. Those kids could be in danger. Contact the plane."

Tong's eyebrows shot up. "Huh?"

"Contact the plane. The pilots were at the hotel. Get the name from them."

Tong grinned. "I like how you think."

Sinai Hospital

Baltimore, Maryland

Rita spotted Sandra Milton through the window of the ER waiting room and rushed inside. Cries were exchanged as Sandra rose and they both embraced each other, sobbing unabashedly. There was nothing shameful on display here today, for while Sandra was Milton's wife, Rita was his work wife.

She loved that man, in an entirely appropriate way.

She had worked for him from the moment he had been named Dean all those years ago, and had served him faithfully day in and day out before handing him back to Sandra at the end of the workday. He always treated her right, never an inappropriate word said or action taken.

He was the perfect boss, and a wonderful man. He loved his students and staff, and was always there for them, sacrificing his own time whenever it was necessary.

And all of this brought back so many memories of when he had been shot, that all she could think about was how changed he had been while stuck in that chair, yet once he had accepted it, how he had been determined to not let it hamper his outlook on life, or how he lived it. And the fact he had been one of the lucky ones who had regained his ability to walk through extremely hard work was a miracle, a miracle she was convinced delivered by Jesus himself for all the good he had done in this world.

Though he would have called her a fool for thinking such things.

"I'm no better than any other man," he would have said, she was certain.

The tearful embrace was finally broken, and she led Sandra back to her seat. "Are you okay?"

Sandra shrugged, clearly not. "What do you think?"

Rita smiled gently at her, quickly straightening the poor woman's disheveled hair, then took a tissue from her purse and wiped away the makeup running from all the tears. "A silly question, I know."

"How'd you find out?"

"One of Jim's neighbors works at the university and someone came to let Greg know. They thought it was Jim that was hurt." She sighed. "Do you know what happened?"

Sandra shook her head. "Not much. Just that he went to check on the house like he normally does when they're away, and somebody I guess was there and did this to him. Somebody, I don't know who, saved him."

"Thank God. What about the person who did this? Did the police arrest him?"

Sandra shrugged. "I don't know. Somebody has him." She stared at Rita. "I don't know how much you know about Jim and Laura, but, well, they have *friends*."

Rita's eyes narrowed. "Friends?"

"The type that, umm…" Sandra shook her head. "It's better you don't know."

Rita's mind was left to fill in the blanks, and none of them were good. Her face must have revealed her fears.

Sandra took her hand. "Oh, they're not bad people! That's not what I meant." She lowered her voice to a whisper. "Think James Bond type stuff."

Rita's eyes widened as her jaw dropped. "Oooh." Her eyes suddenly narrowed. "Is that why they're always off galivanting around the world? They're actually spies?"

Sandra shook her head, patting Rita on the hand. "No." She wagged a finger at her. "And don't say anything to anyone."

Rita ran pinched fingers across her lips. "My lips are sealed." She sighed. "And ironically, this cloak and dagger stuff is why I'm here."

Sandra stared at her. "What do you mean?"

"Well, I hate to ask you this, but there's an emergency. We need to reach somebody named Dylan Kane."

Sandra went pale, paler than she already was. "Dylan? Why? What's going on?"

"The Actons are in trouble, as well as two of their students."

126

"Tommy and Mai?"

Rita's eyes narrowed. "Yes, how did you know?"

Sandra shook her head. "It doesn't matter. Why do they need to reach Dylan?"

"They want to give him the location the professors are heading to before they leave the country." Rita paused. "Who is he? Why is he so important?" Her eyes bulged and she lowered her voice. "Is he one of those *friends* you were talking about?"

Sandra smiled slightly. "I can't say, but unfortunately I have no idea how to reach him."

Rita chewed her cheek for a moment. "Does Greg?"

Sandra nodded. "Yes, I think so, but I don't know if he ever has." Her eyes widened. "But I know who can help!"

Unknown Location, Mongolia

Arban pushed into the corner with his feet as one of the security personnel entered the trailer and marched toward him. The man grabbed him by the arm, the grip viselike, and hauled him to his feet.

"Your boss wants to see you."

Arban said nothing as he was shoved out the door. He stumbled down the few steps to the ground, his captor's grip the only thing saving him from falling. He gasped as a huge backhoe dropped its bucket into a large hole, scooping out a load of dirt near the area the core sample had been taken.

The core sample that had revealed something of potential historical importance.

He spotted Bataar Elbegdor, his boss, nearby, watching the proceedings, and the man smiled at him, beckoning him over. His captor shoved him toward the small group and he reluctantly joined them as rage filled him with each step.

Elbegdor extended an arm and hauled him closer. "Arban, I thought you should see this for yourself. We're almost at the depth the core sample indicated the void should be."

Arban refused to let the man diminish what had been found. "You mean the void with skeletal remains and indications of hand-carved wood."

Elbegdor regarded him for a moment. "Yes, of course." He glanced at the handcuffs. "I'm sorry about this. If only you hadn't run, we might have figured something out. I could have cut you in."

The fire of outrage burned hotter. "No amount of money could ever justify what you're doing."

Elbegdor chuckled. "So young and so naïve. Do you have any idea what this development means for Mongolia? For our people?" He waved his hand, indicating the operation already bigger than anything Arban had witnessed firsthand, and once fully up and running, far larger. "We're talking thousands of jobs, billions upon billions of dollars. A future for our people. This one operation, and those that will follow, could fundamentally alter our country's future."

Arban frowned. "I like our country the way it is. It has its problems, but if your actions here are any indication, all this will do is make those problems worse."

Elbegdor shook his head. "You don't get it, do you? This will inject billions into our economy every year. It will result in thousands of good-paying jobs, and those people will spend that money in our cities and towns, resulting in thousands more in spin-off jobs. We'll finally start to drag the poor out of the gutter and into the middle class, and what is it that the middle class in any country wants?"

Arban shrugged. "I don't know. What?"

"To be like the middle class in America. They want everything the Americans have. That means fancy cars, televisions, computers, cellphones, and the Internet. And once they have that, and realize what else they don't have, they'll want that as well."

Arban stared at him. "What are you talking about?"

"Freedom. Good government. Honest government. Once our people have the money to gain access to the information that has been kept from them merely because they are too poor to access it, they'll see what is wrong with our country, and demand change."

Arban grunted. "So, what you're saying is that *your* greed and corruption is actually saving our country in the long run, so that one day, a man like you can't do what you're doing now."

Elbegdor laughed. "Exactly!"

Arban shook his head. "How do you sleep at night?"

Elbegdor frowned. "Don't think this has come easy for me. I only agreed because I knew eventually they'd find someone who would agree, and that person might not care at all about what might be found. I care. You know that. Look what we're doing here. We're excavating so we can see what was found, and we're doing it properly. Carefully. And if we find something truly significant, it will be preserved."

Arban regarded him for a moment, suddenly confused. "So, you'll shut this down?"

Elbegdor chuckled. "Of course not. But we'll excavate and move whatever we find, should it prove significant, then claim it was discovered elsewhere. Remember, whatever this is can't be very important. It's in the middle of nowhere. Likely, all we'll find is some man who was thrown from his horse, his body left to rot and eventually reclaimed by the elements. A curiosity to be studied in a lab, not hold up the future of a country."

"And if you're wrong?"

"What do you mean?"

"I mean, what if it is significant? Will you change your mind?"

"My boy, I assure you, there is no possibility that what we find here today is of any importance to anyone. And if it proves to be nothing, I might just be able to convince these people to spare your life."

Arban shook his head as he stared at the massive operation. "I'm already dead, sir."

Elbegdor appeared genuinely troubled if his eyes were any indication. "I fear you may be right, but don't lose hope, boy. There's always hope."

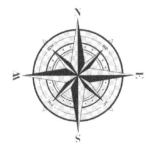

Reading Residence

Whitehall, London, England

Interpol Agent Hugh Reading bolted upright in bed, immediately reaching for the small of his aching back as he cursed at whatever had woken him. His cellphone rang again on his nightstand, and a fresh round of colorful dialog erupted as he rolled over and perched on the edge of his mattress. He unhooked his CPAP mask, the contraption hissing angrily at him before he hit the button to turn it off. He rubbed the sleep out of his eyes as he focused on the number displayed on his phone, finally giving up and just swiping his thumb.

"This better be good," he growled.

"Umm, I'm sorry, but is this Hugh Reading?"

His interest was immediately piqued by the American accent. "Yes. Who is this?"

"My name is Rita Perdok. I'm Dean Gregory Milton's personal assistant."

Now he was fully awake and reached to turn on the lamp then grab his glasses and notepad. "Has something happened to Greg?"

"Yes, as a matter of fact, something has. He was badly beaten in a home invasion earlier today at Professor Acton's house."

Reading's heart raced with concern for his friends. "Are Jim and Laura okay?"

"Well, that's just it. They're in Mongolia, and apparently in some sort of trouble."

He paused his notetaking. "Mongolia? What the bloody hell are they doing there?"

"I have no idea. No one really knows what's going on. Greg is in surgery and his wife is rather distraught. I'm not really sure what to do. Apparently, two of their students are there with them—"

"Tommy and Mai?"

"Yes. You know them?"

"Yes. Why the hell would they take them with them?" He growled again. "Sometimes those two are far more daft than one would think academics should be."

"You'd be surprised at some of the things I see here."

"So, why are you calling me?"

"Well, apparently the professors are heading somewhere that looks to me to be the middle of nowhere, and communications in Mongolia are terrible so there's no way to reach them. Tommy and Mai might have a way of leaving the country shortly, but they don't want to leave without someone named Dylan Kane knowing where the professors are going."

"Where *are* they going?"

"I have GPS coordinates taken from some photo."

"Give them to me." He jotted them down and read them back to confirm. "Okay, so they're heading to these coordinates. Do we know why?"

"I'm not sure. Something about that photograph that showed a hand. I don't know. I'm really confused, and with Greg possibly being crippled again…" She sobbed. "I just don't know what to do!"

Reading's chest tightened at the mention of Milton's condition. "Okay, leave it to me. I know how to reach Dylan. I'll get him the message. If you hear anything else, contact me, okay?"

She sniffed. "Okay, thank you so much."

He ended the call and brought up the secure app Kane had given him in the event he had to be contacted. He sent a message summarizing what he knew, along with the coordinates, then sat wondering what the hell he could do to help the best friends he had in the world. "Get to Mongolia, that's what you can do." He grunted, thinking of the thin ice he was already on at work. "There's no way they'll let you go." He growled and stood. "I'm overdue for retirement anyway!"

Tomorrow was Saturday, so he was off for the next two days regardless. He could at least get in the region as a private citizen using the emergency account Laura had set up for him to use. A sudden wave of guilt washed over him at the thought, but he shoved it aside. Laura was filthy stinking rich, and had set up the account specifically for these situations. For her, this was like him buying a cup of coffee.

Oh, to be rich.

He argued with himself for a few more minutes before literally putting his foot down, leaving him to wonder what people might think if they saw an old copper talking to himself.

Who cares what they bloody think!

His decision was made. If he lost his job, he didn't care. These were his friends and they were in trouble. If there was anything he could do to help, he had to at least try, for if he didn't, and something happened to them, he'd never forgive himself.

Tangut Empire, Western Xia

August 18, 1227 AD

"The Khan is dead."

Wails from the men and women alike filled the outer rooms of the massive tent that housed their leader during his campaigns. It had all the luxuries of a palace, yet all the wealth and opulence on display could do nothing to save the man from the treachery of one young princess.

What a horrible way to die.

It had been an agonizing death, and Mutukan had been there to witness every horrifying moment of it after he returned from his failure to capture the princess responsible.

It had been the only lie he had ever told his master.

"Where is that bitch?"

"She is dead, my master. I killed her myself in a most gruesome fashion."

"I would have preferred to do that myself."

"I know, my master, but in my rage at what she had done, I couldn't help myself. I apologize."

His master dismissed the apology with a wave of his hand. "Forget it. You did well." He grabbed him by the arm, pulling him close. "I'm going to die."

"No, my master, you mustn't speak such things."

"You know it's true. That harpy has gutted me. I can feel it in my bones. My body grows weak." He drew him closer, his voice fading. "You know my wishes."

Mutukan closed his eyes for a moment, his chest aching. "Yes, my master."

"Then I leave it in your hands."

"It will be my honor, my master."

His Khan's grip loosened, his hand finally falling to the bed as his groans of agony continued, the doctors furiously trying to stop the bleeding down below to no avail.

Everyone knew it was already too late.

But no one dared stop, lest they be accused of giving up too soon.

And when he finally passed after hours of agony, the doctors had disappeared within moments, leaving Mutukan alone with his beloved master. He held his Khan's hand tightly against his chest as he sobbed unabashedly in private, the love he had for this man equaled by no other two souls.

He forced himself to let go, to stand like a man, then quickly dressed him, concealing the shame of how he had been killed behind his clothes, then tore the blood-soaked sheets from the bed and piled them in the corner. He straightened the body, folded his master's arms across his chest, then placed his favorite weapons on either side of him.

Then made the pronouncement to those on the other side of the curtains.

"The Khan is dead."

Word swept through the camp, wails of sorrow filling the air for hours, wails that would continue for days. He had immediately ordered word sent to the Khan's sons so the succession could begin, a succession that would be fraught with infighting, for there was disagreement on whether the eldest was a legitimate heir, since his lineage was in question.

The Khan had fathered countless, yet the most important, his eldest son, might not be his.

Yet none of that was his concern. His only concern was that he carry out his master's final wishes.

To be buried in the home of his ancestors, in an unmarked grave, never to be disturbed for eternity.

A massive undertaking.

An undertaking that none could bear witness to.

And live.

East of Ulaanbaatar, Mongolia

Present Day

"Are we being colossally stupid?"

Laura turned from staring off into the distance, the landscape barren and boring, the drive one of the more dull ones they had taken. Even driving the eight hours from Cairo to her dig site in the desert was more exciting—at least there was traffic.

During the entire drive, they had seen perhaps half a dozen cars heading the opposite direction, and none in half an hour. It was tedious, and Acton was exhausted.

"What was that?"

He smiled at his wife, clearly as bored as he was. "I said, are we being colossally stupid?"

"Oh, definitely, but do we have a choice?"

"Of course we do. We could go to the American embassy or the British. They might be able to help."

She pursed her lips. "Yes, I suppose we could, but that won't help Arban."

"True, but an hour ago we were prepared to leave the country and then notify the authorities."

She frowned. "Forgot about that." She eyed him. "So then, why *are* we doing this?"

He grunted. "Well, Hugh would probably say because we're daft, or some other Briticism."

She agreed. "He would that."

"But here's what I'm thinking. Whoever is behind this was foreign and well-equipped."

"Yes, they definitely didn't look local."

"Right. They've proven they don't care about the laws here, so chances are, they don't care about them outside of the country either."

"You mean back home."

"Exactly. And, we know that men like this are expensive, and those photos showed mining core samples. If it's a mining operation, then it's foreign too, because the Mongolians don't have the capability to handle a mine without outside help, and that outside help is almost definitely funding these hired guns."

"I'm with you so far."

"So, I'm thinking we're heading toward a mining operation, a very valuable mining operation, that won't allow anything to stop them, especially some archaeological find."

"Agreed. So, what do you think *we* can do about it?"

"Well, they're in the middle of nowhere, which means I doubt they have much security there. All we need to do is figure out what the name of the company is, and get that info to Dylan. The Feds back home should then be able to get to the bottom of it, and hopefully arrest anyone who might be a threat to us or the kids. Right now, if we head home, we have no idea who is after us, and we could be waiting for a bullet to the back of the head for the rest of our lives, especially once we report what happened to the authorities."

She frowned. "I hadn't thought of that. You're right, of course, it all makes sense when you say it out loud, but I still think this is crazy. We have no support network, and no idea what we're heading into. For all we know, there could be roadblocks ahead with police who've been bribed and told to be on the lookout for us."

He eased off the accelerator. "Huh, that never occurred to me. Do you want to turn back?"

She thought for a moment then shook her head. "No, you're right. As soon as we try to go to the airport, we're going to be arrested or picked up, either by corrupt authorities, or armed mercenaries."

He frowned. "Now you've got me worried about Mai and Tommy."

"Nobody knows they're with us or what they look like. They should be safe." She sighed. "I really don't care what happens to us, I just want them safe."

"Me too. You know, it's funny. I think of those two almost like our son and daughter."

She reached over and patted his leg. "Me too, though perhaps daughter and son-in-law might be less icky."

He laughed. "Good point."

She stared at him, her eyes glistening. "You would have made a great father."

His eyes burned as he patted her hand still on his leg. "And you would have been a fabulous mother."

A tear rolled down her cheek as they both threatened to become overwhelmed by the fact she was unable to have children due to a gunshot wound to the abdomen and the resulting damage.

He forced a smile. "Think of it this way. With Mai and Tommy, we got to avoid the diapers, the tantrums, and the teenage years."

"Not to mention the stretch marks and saggy boobs."

He grinned, giving the girls an ogle. "Wouldn't want that!"

She laughed and punched him gently on the shoulder. "You're terrible."

"Hey, you brought them up."

She sighed. "They're good kids. Let's just hope Mary was able to book a flight and get them the info. For all we know, they could already be on their way to the airport."

Kempinski Hotel Khan Palace

Ulaanbaatar, Mongolia

Tommy stared at the text message that had just arrived, forcing the decision they had both been putting off. Mai stopped her pacing.

"What is it?"

"It's from the travel agent. She's got four seats booked on a flight in two hours, but we have to leave now if we're going to make it."

Mai stared at their luggage by the door. "What do we do?"

Tommy sighed, foolishly playing the man card. "You should go. Get out of here while you can. I'll stay to make sure our message got to Dylan."

Mai shoved her hands onto her hips. "Don't be all chivalrous on me. Besides, we got the coordinates to Dean Milton's secretary. It's her responsibility now. We both have to go, and we have to go now while we can. The longer we stay, the more likely it is that someone will discover we're here."

Tommy chewed his cheek, staring at her. She was right. The coordinates were now outside the country, which had always been his concern. If they were arrested at the airport, then no one would ever know where the professors had gone. But now that Rita had them, she would get them to Milton, and he could get them to Kane. His job was done.

Their job was done.

"You're right. Let's get the hell out of here." He snapped his laptop shut and rolled out of bed, shoving the device into one of the pouches on his carry-on. "Have we got everything?"

"I've checked a hundred times."

He chuckled, giving her a quick kiss. "I know you have."

He opened the door and Mai cried out as he gasped, three large men with insincere smiles blocking their paths.

"Going somewhere?"

Operations Center 3, CIA Headquarters
Langley, Virginia

Leroux stared at the screen uselessly, little of the intel displayed current. He turned to Child. "ETA on our operative?"

"Five minutes."

Leroux growled then returned to his station. It had been a bit of a chore to contact the pilot, the nightshift at the charter not believing them at first. When Child hacked their system and let them watch as he extracted the information himself, Leroux had asked the simple question.

"Do you believe me now?"

"Yes?"

"And we have your permission to contact the pilot?"

"Umm, yes?"

And the call had been made, the location of the crew's hotel provided, and the confirmation given that local police had shown up at the hotel and escorted them directly to the airport without the rest of the crew or their luggage.

Tong turned in her chair to face him. "This is interesting."

"What?"

"I've been monitoring airline bookings like you asked, and a bunch of them just showed up for the professors and their students."

Child spun in his chair, staring at the ceiling. "That travel agent is definitely on the ball."

"Yeah, four seats on half a dozen flights, all spaced out by roughly half a day."

Leroux smiled at the resourcefulness shown. "When's the first flight?"

"Less than two hours from now."

"Is there any indication they've checked in?"

Tong shook her head. "No. The flights were only booked in the past half hour."

Leroux rose. "If the travel agent was able to get this information to them, then they might just get themselves out of the country. Maybe." He tapped her monitor. "Get that info to our guy. He can take them to the airport and put them on that flight himself if he has to."

Tong's fingers flew over the keyboard. "Done." She looked up at him. "Umm, I've got something else you're not going to like."

His eyes narrowed. "What now?"

"Well, on a whim, I added a few more names to the search, and a ticket was just booked from London to Seoul."

Leroux sighed and returned to his station, collapsing in his chair. "Let me guess. Agent Reading of Interpol?"

"Yup."

He shook his head. "The professors have too many friends willing to do whatever it takes."

Tong regarded him. "Doesn't that include us?"

Leroux grunted. "I suppose it does. When does his flight leave?"

"In two hours."

"Good. Then he should still be answering his phone. Get him for me."

Kempinski Hotel Khan Palace

Ulaanbaatar, Mongolia

Stander stepped into the hotel room as their two targets retreated toward the window. Once he had figured out that the professors had smuggled them in as flight crew, finding them was a simple matter.

And could prove fruitful, as he was quite certain the professors would turn themselves over the moment they found out these two were in his custody.

"Very clever what your friends did. Irresponsible, but clever. I mean, they're old enough to be your parents, yet they bring you to Mongolia of all places. They must not like you very much."

The girl opened her mouth to no doubt defend the professors, but the boy wisely cut her off. "What do you want?"

"I want the professors."

"They're not here."

"No, I'm sure they're not, but I'm sure they told you where they were going."

"How could they? We haven't seen them since the airplane."

Stander shook his head, mock disappointment on his face. "I really hate it when I'm lied to. I mean, if everyone just told the truth, the world would be a much better place."

"More boring though," said Myburg.

Stander chuckled "Yes, more boring, but better." He stepped closer and the boy herded the girl behind him.

Boyfriend and girlfriend? That could be useful.

"Now, I need to know where the professors are, and you don't want to tell me. I know you know, because the hotel staff I bribed told me they were here earlier. They wouldn't leave here without telling you where they were going." He gestured at their luggage. "Now, where were you going? To meet them?"

"No, we're just going to the airport to catch a flight home. That's all they told us. They said to wait for a text message from the travel agent, then go to the airport and get on the flight. That's all I know, I swear."

Stander smiled slightly. "Oh, you swear? Then it must be the truth."

"It is!" cried the girl.

Stander stepped closer and the boy stepped back, bumping into the girl. "Thomas is it? And Mai?"

The boy went pale. "H-how do you know that?"

"The crew manifest. Like I said. Very clever. Nobody ever watches the crew. If you've got a flight out of here, then that means whoever booked it could have booked it for all four of you. The fact the professors aren't here means they had somewhere else to be. And that concerns me, because it concerns my client. Now, I don't like being concerned. I like being in complete control of every situation. And so, when I'm not in control, I do whatever it takes to get in control." He swiftly drew his weapon and swung his arm toward Tommy, stopping over the boy's shoulder, the barrel aimed squarely at the young woman cowering behind her boyfriend. "Tell me everything you know, right now, or I promise you my men will have their way with her all night while you watch, then we'll put a bullet in her head."

Jack—just Jack—parked his Camry about a hundred yards short of the hotel where the two subjects Langley was interested in were staying. As he walked to the entrance, he spotted an SUV idling nearby, a vehicle far nicer than most in the city. And shook his head at the driver—Caucasian with short-clipped hair.

Do you have to be so obvious about it?

At least he now knew he was heading into a situation, and with only one vehicle in sight, he was probably up against three to five well-trained men. This wouldn't be easy. In fact, it could prove impossible.

"I should have been a brain surgeon."

He suppressed a chuckle at the phrase, something his instructor at The Farm had said repeatedly every time a recruit frustrated him. He had adopted the mantra as his own, though had never spoken the words aloud.

Until today.

I wonder if that means something.

He might be dead in the next five minutes, which would be unfortunate, though he wouldn't be missed. Jobs like this were usually given to those with few connections, especially family. He had no wife, no kids, no siblings, no parents—no living parents.

And no friends.

It was a lonely life. And that was exactly how he liked it. Nobody to hurt you. Nobody to betray you. Do the job, and if, at the end of the day you were still alive, then you probably did it right. And if you weren't, then what did it matter? He didn't believe in all that Heaven and Hell crap. You were alive, and then you weren't.

End of story.

He entered the lobby and spotted a suitable employee. He pulled a pre-written note from his pocket, a month's wages tucked inside, and handed it to him, giving him a look.

"Five minutes?"

The young man's eyes bulged at the cash then he quickly read the note and nodded. Jack scanned the lobby for his subjects and any hostiles, finding nothing. It meant they were either on their way down, or still in the room, about to be on their way down. And with only one elevator, currently on the second floor, and his subjects on the fourth, it was a safe bet they were in the room.

He pressed the button and the elevator arrived moments later. He gripped his weapon, tucked in his belt underneath his jacket, and was greeted with an empty cab. He stepped inside and pressed the button for the third floor, riding up in silence, the chime indicating he had arrived, the doors opening then closing a few moments later.

And he waited.

Though not for long.

The elevator jerked and headed up. He drew his weapon, screwing the suppressor in place, and readied himself. He was about to either scare the living shit out of some poor tourist, or get the drop on superior numbers. The doors opened on the fourth floor and he squeezed the trigger.

Tommy's eyes bulged and Mai screamed as a man fired over Tommy's shoulder then over his other, dropping two of their kidnappers before they could react. A hand reached out and grabbed Mai by the shirt, yanking her inside the elevator. Tommy reached out to stop her as the man in charge, the man he had just spilled everything to only moments ago without a finger laid on him, dove out of the way, drawing his weapon and swinging it toward them.

Tommy's jaw dropped as he realized there was only one possible target left and he dove into the elevator with Mai and a man his mind hadn't yet had a chance to classify as friend or foe. Gunfire erupted behind him, tearing into the door as the new arrival hammered on the Close Door button, Lobby already lit. The man reached out with his left hand and corralled them to the opposite side of the elevator then dropped to a knee, aiming at the opening. Tommy spotted a shadow and their rescuer—for he was now certain that's who he was—fired two rounds before the door finally closed and the elevator began its descent.

He reloaded and glanced at them. "You two okay?"

Tommy shook out a nod. "Y-yes. Who-who are you?"

"Call me Jack. Some friends stateside sent me to make sure you got on a plane. Looks like I got here just in time."

"Yeah, uh, thanks."

"Don't thank me yet, kid, we ain't out of this shitstorm until you two are wheels up. There's still one upstairs, and there was one outside, and I have no doubt they have comms. Here's the plan. You two hug that wall like it was your lover, and then stick to my ass and do everything I tell you. No hesitation. This is still going to be ugly."

The chime had Tommy's heart pumping hard and he pressed himself against Mai and her against the wall as the door opened, Jack dropping to a knee again, two shots fired as a single round shattered the mirror behind them.

"Let's go!"

Tommy grabbed Mai by the hand and they followed Jack out of the elevator, the man's head on a swivel as he searched for more trouble. Tommy didn't bother looking. It was everything he could do to not faint and to keep hold of Mai's hand. They reached the revolving doors, an employee handing Jack something as their savior shoved them through, apparently confident no one was outside.

Jack stepped through and pointed toward a car. "Back seat. Both of you, then get down."

Tommy nodded and they raced toward the non-descript Toyota. He opened the rear door and Mai leaped inside, her entire body shaking as he followed suit, closing the door as Jack fired up the engine. Gunfire rang out and Jack grabbed some sort of machine gun, Tommy wasn't sure, from the passenger seat and stuck it out the window, the deafening roar of the fully automatic weapon sending them both cringing to the floor, and apparently their kidnapper diving for cover, for moments later they were turning a corner, the hotel out of sight.

"Okay, kids, you can relax now. We're going to switch vehicles, then head straight for the airport. You're getting on that flight they booked for you, and within a few hours you'll be in South Korea. From there you're on your own. Just call Mom and Dad and I'm sure they'll get you home."

"But we don't have our passports! The hotel took them!" cried Mai. "They'll never let us on board!"

Jack handed them an envelope, the same envelope Tommy had noticed the employee hand over as they left the hotel. "Here you go."

Tommy opened the envelope and smiled at Mai at the sight of their passports. This plan seemed to be coming together. He checked his watch. And they still had time.

Something occurred to him. "We don't have luggage. Won't that look suspicious?"

Jack grinned at him over his shoulder. "Don't worry, kid, it's all taken care of."

Heathrow Airport

London, England

Hugh Reading sat impatiently at his gate, waiting for boarding to begin. He had taken the plunge and bought the ticket, yelping out loud at the price, the only seat left in business class.

It's two cups of coffee for her.

He had repeated that half a dozen times before clicking to accept the price, printing off his itinerary the moment it arrived in his inbox. He had let his son know through a text message where he was going and generally why—the young man was a copper now and had also dealt with the Actons' exploits, so he trusted him to be able to handle it.

But he had told no one else.

That was why he was surprised his phone was vibrating in his pocket at this ungodly hour of the morning. He checked the call display, not recognizing the number, and debated on whether to answer.

Well, it's not the office.

He swiped his thumb. "Hello?"

"Agent Reading, this is Chris, an associate of a mutual friend named Dylan."

He frowned. "Yes, Chris, I know who you are. And if you're calling me, then things are obviously worse than I've been fearing."

Leroux chuckled. "Yes, I'm usually the bearer of bad tidings. May I ask why you're going to Seoul?"

Reading's eyes narrowed. "Didn't Dylan tell you?"

"We've been out of communication with him for several hours. Why? Have you been in contact?"

Reading looked about to make sure he was alone. He was, at least as far as Heathrow would allow. "Tommy Granger got a set of GPS coordinates to Greg Milton's secretary, and she got them to me. I sent them to Dylan along with everything she told me."

"What did she tell you?"

"That Jim and Laura were heading to these coordinates, that the coordinates were taken from some photo—what was in that photo, or where they got it, she didn't know or remember. What do you know?"

"Less than you, apparently. I'm going to need those coordinates."

"Hold on." Reading retrieved the piece of paper he had written the coordinates on and read them off. Leroux repeated them then whistled as he apparently entered them in his computer.

"Middle of nowhere Mongolia."

"Exactly. I checked Google and couldn't find anything there. Do you guys have any updated imagery?"

"Of course not." There was a pause. "It looks like some sort of mining operation. Open pit. Fairly big, but looks like it's set to expand. Any idea why they'd head there?"

"None."

"Does Arban Namjiliin mean anything to you?"

Reading's eyebrows rose. "No. Is that some kind of religious headdress?"

Leroux laughed. "It's a name, Agent Reading. Apparently, he sent a text message to Professor Acton, telling him he was in trouble and someone was trying to kill him. They then promptly boarded an airplane, along with Thomas Granger and Mai Trinh—"

"*That* I can't believe!"

"Yeah, we were puzzled by that too. They snuck them in as flight crew. We have an asset retrieving them now. We're assuming they needed Mr. Granger's computer expertise, and that Miss Trinh insisted on accompanying him."

Reading shook his head. "She gets that from her mentors. Neither of those two will go anywhere without the other if it's dangerous. Do you know if Jim and Laura are okay?"

"No, we have no information on their status, though it's likely they are indeed heading to the coordinates you provided."

"Is there anything you can do?"

"We're working it. I recommend you stay in London, sir. There's nothing you can do to help them."

Reading grunted. "I'll take it under advisement."

He could hear Leroux's exasperated sigh. "Fine, we'll monitor your phone for when you arrive in Seoul."

Reading laughed. "You do that."

En route to Genghis Khan International Airport

Ulaanbaatar, Mongolia

Jack's watch pulsed a signal to his wrist and he grabbed his phone, reading the secure message that had just arrived. He shook his head then looked in the rearview mirror.

"So, your professor friends are heading to some strip mine in the middle of nowhere?"

Tommy's eyes widened. "That's what it is?"

"If those coordinates are correct."

Tommy smiled at Mai then leaned forward between the seats. "So, Dylan got our message?"

"Somebody did."

"Oh, thank God! What are you going to do?"

"I'm getting you two out of the country. When I've accomplished that, then I'll deal with the next problem."

Mai squeezed forward. "But they could be in danger!"

Jack shrugged. "They've got a long drive ahead of them. The biggest danger they have at this moment is a flat tire or a roadblock, neither of which I can help them with once it becomes a problem. Right now, we've got armed gunmen who actively want you dead."

Tommy went pale. "What makes you say that? They didn't kill us."

"That was because they had you, and wanted to take you somewhere where they could make sure they knew everything you did. Now that you've been compromised, the smart thing to do is kill you."

Mai's face clouded with fear. "Is that what you would do?"

He hated the answer that came from his mouth. "Without hesitation."

Tommy groaned, sitting back. "Lovely. And you're supposed to be one of the good guys."

Jack chuckled. "It's all a matter of whose side of the equation you're on, kid. Right now, I'm on your side, they're not." They pulled up to the airport drop-off zone. "Now, your new luggage is in the trunk. You've got your passports. Just go inside, act normal, and pick up your tickets. Go through security as soon as you can, go to your gate, and get on your flight. Don't talk to anyone unless they're staff. Anyone else, just pretend you don't speak the language. Don't talk to each other. I find pretending to be asleep helps. Just don't actually fall asleep and miss your flight. Stay calm, and you'll be fine. Remember, you've done nothing wrong. The bad guys are all outside."

Tommy gripped Mai's hand. "What about the authorities?"

Jack shook his head. "That all depends on how deep the pockets go that are involved, and if they've had time to get your information to their

160

contacts. My guess is you're okay, since everything has gone down in the past few minutes." He jerked a thumb toward the terminal. "Now go! You've got ninety minutes."

Leaving Kempinski Hotel Khan Palace

Ulaanbaatar, Mongolia

Stander pulled away from the hotel as his phone connected with the SUV's Bluetooth. Curses sputtered from his mouth as he slammed his fist repeatedly into the dash before grabbing his phone. His men were dead, a mess left behind, and worse, the targets had escaped. Whoever had rescued them was good.

Too good.

That meant professional, possibly an intelligence operative. It had to be CIA or something equivalent. But that made no sense. Why the hell would the CIA come rescue two kids? Who were these people? How connected were they? He had to know more, and right now the professors were God knows where, the kids were probably getting on a flight out of the country, and he was no closer to knowing what was actually going on.

It was unfamiliar territory for him, and it was driving him mad. He needed intel, but all he knew from his extensive contacts was that Mai Trinh was a Vietnamese citizen living in exile in the United States—and no one knew why. Thomas Granger was a former hacker gone straight. James Acton was a professor who had made the news several times for being in the wrong place at the wrong time, and was former National Guard. And his wife, Laura Palmer, was rich through an inheritance received from her late brother, and also made the news a few times, always with her husband.

His mouth slowly opened as he realized a possibility. She was rich. Fabulously rich, apparently, and that could mean private security. They might already be here, in place, though they definitely hadn't come in on the charter flight. That could be who rescued the kids and killed his men. His head slowly bobbed at the possibility. It was far preferable than dealing with the CIA or some other spy agency's assets.

It didn't solve his problem, though his problem just might solve itself. Tommy had given him the coordinates that the professors were heading to, and he already knew the destination. The mine. All they had to do was wait for them to show up, and then they'd have them.

One problem soon to be resolved.

The next was the bigger one. Who knew what? The two kids obviously knew something, and they'd have to be dealt with stateside. He chewed his cheek for a moment.

Unless palms could be quickly greased.

He swiped his thumb and dialed his contact.

Mine Site, Eastern Mongolia

Arban watched the excavator continue its work, the depth of the curiosity discovered in the core sample almost reached. The going was slow in the dark with his corrupt asshat of a boss at least appearing to take care in not damaging whatever the void might contain. But they were running out of time.

A phone rang and Elbegdor answered it, the one-sided conversation begun within earshot, but finished outside of it when Elbegdor noticed him listening. His boss returned a few minutes later.

"Killing more innocent people?" asked Arban, pushing his luck.

"It's none of your concern."

"I suppose not, since I'm dead anyway. You're married. You have kids. How can you go home at the end of the day and look them in the eye knowing what you've done?"

Elbegdor regarded him. "With ease."

Arban's eyes shot wide. "Excuse me? With ease?"

"Yes, with ease. I know that what I am doing here will result in a more prosperous Mongolia, and that means a better future for my children." He regarded Arban for a moment. "And I told you, never give up hope. There's still a chance you'll get out of here alive, go back to your wife, make babies, and know that someday they'll have a better life than yours because of what happens here tonight."

Arban grunted. "You're mad."

"No, I'm a realist. Like I said before, if it wasn't me here, it would be someone else. The only difference is they might not care what we find here tonight. I do. If it is important, it will be preserved, and the mine will continue its expansion. This resource is simply too valuable, too important. Without it, entire economies could fail, wars could be fought over it."

Arban shook his head. "Has it ever occurred to you that it could make us a target? Have you looked at a map lately? We're trapped between Russia and China, essentially two of the most immoral countries on the planet today. It's not as if the Americans are going to leap to our defense if one of them decides to cross the border and take what they want."

Elbegdor shook his head. "No, you're wrong. With this properly developed, the clout we will have on the world stage will be immense, and the West who are desperate for it will protect us. Yes, the Chinese or the Russians might invade, but the real weapon today is trade. Sanctions, tariffs, barriers. Neither country would dare invade because they'd know their economies would be crippled if they did."

"You're taking one hell of a risk with our nation's future."

"Thinking like that, my boy, would mean no one would risk anything, and there'd be no progress outside of those with militaries mighty enough to protect their economic interests. We must take the risk, forge on, and build a more prosperous nation. I really wish you could see the good that will come of this. If I could just convince you, I know I could convince those in charge to spare your life."

Arban turned away and stared at the excavator. Was he willing to die for his principles? All he had to do was trick Elbegdor into thinking he was on his side, that he had been swayed, and he just might see his wife again, just might have those babies they had been planning, and then grow old and fat, and in twenty or thirty years see if Elbegdor had been right. It was appealing, obviously, but it also made him sick to his stomach.

Does Badma deserve to be left alone because of your principles?

Elbegdor was right. No matter what, this mine was moving forward. Even if he had successfully got the word out, the government was corrupt. Officials would be bribed, the story buried, misinformation spread, and soon it would be dismissed as fake news, if his limited experience with the modern way of life was any indication.

The truth didn't matter, it was who controlled the medium meant to spread it that did.

He drew a deep breath, deciding he had no choice. He turned to Elbegdor. "You promise that if we find something, it will be preserved properly?"

Elbegdor smiled. "You have my word."

Heathrow Airport

London, England

"Are you sure?"

Reading wasn't sure at all, so he understood his partner's confusion. This wasn't any ordinary request, and could get them both in hot water if things went south. "Yes. But don't put them in the system yet. Just get them ready in case I need them. I don't want any delays once I pull the trigger."

"You're going to get fired for this for sure. And so am I for helping you."

Reading chuckled. "They won't fire you. They like you. Me? I'm long overdue to be given the boot. Besides, I'll tell them I lied to you."

Michelle Humphrey laughed. "They won't believe you."

"Okay, I used your user ID to access the system and did it myself."

"Ha! They'd believe that only if they thought you could use a computer."

"Haw haw." He thought for a moment. "That's actually a good idea. When I tell you to pull the trigger, do it remotely then deny knowing anything about it. I don't want you getting in trouble, but this might just save their lives, and two of them are just kids."

Michelle sighed. "I knew when I was partnered with you, you'd be trouble."

He smiled. "Yes, but living on the edge is more exciting, isn't it?"

"It is, but if I wanted excitement, I never would have joined Interpol."

He laughed. "Good point. So, will you do it?"

"Consider it done, Hugh. But when you get back, you're buying the pints."

"Deal!"

Genghis Khan International Airport

Ulaanbaatar, Mongolia

Tommy gulped as he spotted half a dozen armed men approaching in the distance. He stood, pushing Mai back into her seat without looking, then moved to the next row of seats. He sat and closed his eyes, feigning sleep like Jack had suggested.

The hammering of boots on the tile floor were almost in unison, each clap of rubber on stone sending his heart beating faster, and he had to stop from squeezing his eyes shut like a child hiding from the monsters under his bed.

Shouts erupted and he flinched, his eyes shooting wide open, there no point in feigning sleep anymore, as no one could through the racket.

And his jaw dropped.

A young couple, both Asian, were surrounded, automatic weapons pointed at them from all directions, something in Mongolian shouted at them by the man in charge, the only words he understood being Thomas Granger and Mai Trinh.

Four more words than the two passengers they were directed at, passengers obviously not locals as they appeared to have no idea what was being said. They merely raised their hands, both pale, both trembling with fear, before they were hauled to their feet and cuffed, then led quickly away.

It was over in seconds, and Thomas looked around, making a point to not make eye contact with Mai, though making certain she was still in her seat out of the corner of his eye.

A gong sounded and the gate attendant announced that boarding had now started. He stood, heading for the gate slowly, making certain Mai was ahead of him. As long as she made it safely on board, he didn't care what happened to him. But as they cleared the gate, a tremendous wave of guilt washed over him at the thought of what might be happening to the two poor souls who had just been arrested, merely for the crime of generally matching their description—young, and sitting together at the same gate.

As soon as we're safe, I'll try to get word to someone who can help.

Ulaanbaatar, Mongolia

"We have them. What do you want me to do with them?"

Stander smiled at the news, his contact, Captain Ganhuyag, having come through at the last minute. "Nothing. I'll come pick them up."

"You have my money?"

"Not on me, but you'll get it. You know I'm good for it."

"No money, no prisoners."

Stander resisted the instinct to yell as he put his SUV in gear. "The money is at the mine. Have I ever let you down?"

There was a pause. "Fine. But the price is double."

"Bullshit. I'll give you an extra ten percent."

"Fifty."

"Twenty. Final offer."

"Fine. When do you want to meet?"

"Ten minutes, the usual place."

"I'll be there. But I want my money by end of day tomorrow."

171

"You'll have it."

Stander headed for the rendezvous just outside of the city, and dialed his client. "We've got the kids."

"So, good news for a change. Are they dead yet?"

Stander shook his head.

Again with the rush decisions.

"No. I want a chance to interrogate them. I'm picking them up now. I'll bring them to the site on the chopper. Oh, and we'll have to add twenty percent to the usual payoff. Ganhuyag got a little greedy."

There was a displeased sigh through the speakers. "I don't mind corruption, but I hate greed. It might be time to find a replacement."

"I'll look into it. And if I find one?"

"Once he proves reliable, Mr. Ganhuyag should have an accident."

"Understood. I'll be there within an hour in time for our professors to arrive. We should have this entire situation cleared up by morning."

"Good. We're going to have to be more careful from now on. We're too deep into this to allow locals with a conscience to risk an operation this size."

Stander shrugged as he made a turn. "I told you having them there was a mistake."

"We had to make it look at least reasonably legitimate. Who the hell would have thought we'd have ever found something here? We're in the middle of nowhere, and we find a damned body? It's insane!"

Stander spotted his contact ahead, the headlights flashing twice. "Okay, I'm about to pick up the kids. I'll call you when I'm in the air."

Stander ended the call as he pulled behind Ganhuyag's vehicle. "Taban! How's the family?"

Ganhuyag smiled, extending a hand. "My eldest son is going to university in Beijing, thanks to you. He starts in September."

Stander shook the man's hand then wiped the sweat on his pant leg. "Glad to hear it. You keep working with us, and he'll be a doctor before you know it."

Ganhuyag beamed then opened the rear door of his vehicle. "As requested, your rodent problem, solved." He beckoned for the passengers to get out and Stander stepped back as they struggled from the rear seat, both still cuffed.

Then cursed when Ganhuyag shone his flashlight in their faces.

"That's not them!"

Ganhuyag's eyes bulged. "What?"

"That's not them! Thomas Granger is a white American for crying out loud! This kid is Asian!"

"How the hell was I supposed to know? You said an American boy and a Vietnamese girl. Americans can be anything. You never said white! And they were sitting together at the right gate, they didn't deny who they were! How the hell was I supposed to know?"

Stander turned to the prisoners. "What are your names?"

They stared at him with narrowed eyes, shaking their heads as they sobbed something in what sounded like Chinese. Stander cursed and spun back toward his SUV.

What the hell do I do now?

He checked his watch. The flight was already gone. That meant his targets were out of reach until they landed. But now he had two innocents here that would ask questions, had seen his face, and that of his contact within the government. If Ganhuyag were to be implicated in this, he'd spill the beans with the first raised voice, then the entire operation could come tumbling down.

He shook his head. There was only one option.

He drew his weapon and turned. "Sorry about this." He fired two rounds into Ganhuyag's chest, the man dropping before he could make a sound. The girl screamed and the boy selflessly put himself between her and the gun.

Stander hesitated. Were they really a risk to him?

The girl ran.

He put two in her back then two in her boyfriend's chest. He holstered his weapon, shaking his head. If she had just given him time to think. He shrugged.

Wrong place, wrong time, kids.

Khentii Region, Mongol Empire

1227 AD

There had been rumors, of course, and with so few having seen what had happened, their source was obvious.

The doctors.

Mutukan had immediately ordered their execution, along with any that worked with them, and taken it upon himself to regale the men at the end of each day about the heroic ferocity of their late leader as he had charged into battle, ignoring the arrow embedded in his leg that would eventually take his life, instead continuing to lead, to slaughter the enemy, then behead the leaders that had dared to defy the mighty Mongol Empire.

And it had worked.

The word spread among the burial party, thirty thousand strong, as it headed back to their homeland, slaughtering any who caught sight of the procession.

For no one could know their final destination.

No one.

Thousands of innocents had died along the way, though they were close now.

In fact, they were here.

He held up his fist, bringing the entire procession to a halt as he gazed out ahead of him at the long stretch of flat land in front of them, a river to the east, mountains to the north, and not a soul in sight.

It was perfect.

He turned to the general in command of the army, the burial the only thing a slave like Mutukan could be in charge of. "This is it."

The general smiled. "A good choice. He would be pleased."

The order was given, and the procession set up camp as Mutukan took his horse ahead to find the perfect spot. As he rode slowly along the peaceful terrain, he spotted something on the ground and stopped. He dismounted and took a knee, prying loose a large flat stone, wiping it free of the dirt caked on it.

And knew it was a sign from his master.

This was the place.

Eastern Mongolia

Present Day

"It's definitely got to be some sort of mine."

Laura jerked awake. "Huh?"

"Where we're headed. It has to be some sort of mine. I mean, what else could it be? Most things require a workforce. The only time you put an operation where there's no nearby workforce is when you're dealing with natural resources. You have to bring the workers to the resource. It has to be a mine. Nobody kills over trees."

She stretched, a contented moan escaping before settling back into her seat. "I thought we had already decided it was?"

Acton shrugged. "You know me. I like to rehash things, just to make sure."

She chuckled. "Makes sense. Mines are billion-dollar operations. More, depending upon what they're mining and how big a find they have. I could see someone killing over that kind of operation."

Acton chewed his cheek. "We're about halfway there. Here's what I'm thinking. Next place we see, gas station, restaurant, whatever, I drop you off, I go get the info we need—"

She held up a finger. "Let me stop you right there. You think I'd be safer as a woman, alone, in the middle of nowhere in Mongolia, than with you?"

Acton stared at her for a moment before returning his attention to the empty road. "Yeah, sometimes I wonder how I became a professor."

"Because there were no courses in dealing with killers."

He flashed her a grin. "That's my girl, always leaping to my defense."

She returned the grin and squeezed his leg. "Nobody picks on my guy." She ran her hand up his leg. "You know, it's a long drive."

His eyes widened. "Yeess?"

"Well, I was thinking, we're in the middle of nowhere. We could pull over, relieve some stress, and just drive a little faster and get there at the same time."

He laughed. "Babe, you'll have to drive then, because I'll be all sleepy once we're done."

She shrugged. "I'm game."

Acton was about to pull over when he heard something behind them. He stared in his rearview mirror and cursed.

Operations Center 3, CIA Headquarters

Langley, Virginia

Child spun in his chair. "I've confirmed it. Tommy and Mai boarded the plane and it's cleared Mongolian airspace. They should be on the ground in Seoul shortly."

Leroux smiled, turning to the team. "That's two down, people, two to go. As soon as they clear Chinese airspace and are over international waters, contact our embassy and have them met at the airport."

Child's eyes narrowed. "You really think the Chinese would try something?"

Leroux shrugged. "Who knows, but why take the risk? Have we been able to figure out who owns that mine yet?"

Tong shook her head. "Not yet. I've gone over the satellite imagery and there appears to be no signage whatsoever. It's like whoever is there doesn't want anyone to know who they are."

"Government-run?" suggested Child.

"No way, not there."

Leroux returned to his station. "Okay, check the archives and see when this thing first showed up, then check to see if there were any press reports of mining rights being granted around that time. This is a massive operation. Somebody has to have mentioned it in their annual reports to their shareholders."

"Got it." Tong returned to her keyboard then paused. "Oh, and boss, somebody else is in the air."

Leroux shook his head. "Of course he is. That man is as bad as the professors."

"They *are* good friends. Wouldn't you drop everything to help a friend?"

The room stopped to look at Leroux and he shook his head. "No. I'd send Delta, then sit back and take the credit."

Laughter erupted and Leroux mentally patted himself on the back for the save.

Mine Site, Eastern Mongolia

Arban was fully committed to the deception now, but not for the reason of self-preservation. The excavator had finished, and now the shovel work was beginning, otherwise they risked damaging whatever was in the void they had discovered. He had studied to be an anthropologist, his specialty Mongolian history, specifically that of the Mongol Empire.

Mongolia's history was a tremendous source of pride among its people, despite Soviet efforts to stamp it out with their demongolization policy, yet it was also a constant reminder of what had been lost. Once the Mongol armies ruled one of the largest swaths of land in history, extending from Eastern Europe to the Pacific, including most of modern China and Russia, and now they were confined to a landlocked country that few in the world could find on a map.

He frowned. Perhaps Elbegdor was right. Perhaps having a mine like this in operation, and the prosperity it would bring, was a good thing.

And if they had found nothing, would he have objected? Of course not. He was here. Happily, until yesterday.

And the past day had given him plenty of time to second guess his actions. Stander had put his hand on his weapon. Maybe it was simply an affectation. Maybe it had meant nothing. Yet he had run, creating a situation, or making a situation worse. They might have simply let things play out to see what they had found. Instead, he had acted on his principles, and now he had been beaten, and involved other innocents by sending that text message.

This was all his fault.

Yet none of it mattered now. For now, he was playing archaeologist, something he loved, and was determined to do the best job they would let him do. And if he played his cards right, he just might be allowed to live, or if that weren't an option, perhaps Acton's contacts might save him before it was too late.

For there was little doubt his old teacher had done something that had everyone concerned.

He grabbed a bundle of stakes, a mallet, and a spool of twine, then turned to Elbegdor. "Shall we?"

Elbegdor smiled as if the past 24 hours had never occurred. "Let's!"

Eastern Mongolia

Laura stared behind them, her eyes bulging at the sight of a helicopter racing toward them, silhouetted against the night sky and a nearly full moon. It appeared to be almost scraping the pavement as it rushed toward them.

We're going to die!

The car surged forward as James hit the accelerator and she turned toward him. "You're going to try and outrun them?"

He eased up, though her pounding heart didn't. "What should I do?"

She stared, uncertain. What *could* they do? "Stop before they shoot?"

He sighed, nodding, then slowly brought them to a halt as the helicopter passed overhead, its massive rotors pounding the air above them, the entire car shaking. She watched in horror as it banked to face them, then slowly settled onto the ground, heavily armed soldiers pouring out either side then racing toward them, their weapons raised.

Within moments they were surrounded, orders shouted at them in a language neither of them understood, though the intent was clear.

They wanted them out of the car.

"Do you think they're going to kill us?"

James frowned as he raised his hands. She did the same as one soldier on either side of the car stepped forward and tried to open the doors, doors the car had automatically locked the moment they began to drive two hours earlier. Angry shouts followed the failed attempts and Laura yelped as the butt of an AK-47 smashed her window. She leaned away from the shattered glass, James grabbing her and covering her as the same was done to his window.

The doors were pulled open and hands gripped her, yanking her into the chill of the night. "James!" she cried as she was thrown painfully to the ground before being hauled to her feet.

"I'm okay! Just stay calm!"

"Yes, just stay calm," said a voice, American by the sounds of it. Laura squinted into the bright lights of the helicopter, trying to find the source of the first words she had understood since this ordeal began, finally spotting a man stepping between the soldiers, a smile on his face, his civilian clothes casual. "I assume you are Professors Acton and Palmer?"

"Who wants to know?" asked James, Laura suppressing a smile at the defiance in her husband's voice.

"You can call me Jack. Friends of yours from Langley sent me."

Laura smiled, sighing with relief, her arms slowly lowering.

Thank God, we're safe!

A soldier emerged from the blinding lights, dressed differently than the others, clearly an officer, probably in charge. Words were exchanged in Mongolian, then orders barked, half a dozen of the weapons suddenly aimed at Jack.

Who cursed as he slowly raised his hands, looking at the two people he was supposed to save. "Sorry about this, but it would appear we're the victims of the old double-cross cliché."

Operations Center 3, CIA Headquarters

Langley, Virginia

"Play that back?"

Tong complied and everyone in the room stopped to listen.

"Sorry about this, but it would appear we're the victims of the old double-cross cliché."

Leroux shook his head. "Did he just say what I think he said?"

Child spun in his chair. "If he sounds like he just found out they weren't joking about the final season of Game of Thrones, then yes, I think he did."

Leroux cursed as Director Leif Morrison entered the operations center.

"I've had better greetings."

Leroux chuckled. "Sorry, sir, that wasn't meant for you." He motioned at the screens curving across the front of the room. "Our little op in Mongolia just went south."

"Our Mongolian military contacts weren't helpful?"

"Oh, they were helpful, just for the wrong side. It looks like they pulled a fast one on our contact just as they caught up to the professors."

It was Morrison's turn to curse. "You mean the Mongolian military has our operative, plus two civilians, including an American citizen and a British citizen?"

Leroux nodded at the purposefully detailed question.

"And from that briefing note you just sent me, we believe that this mine was started two years ago by FirstPrime Mining, which is a massive multinational that is listed on the New York Stock Exchange, with headquarters in Seattle?"

"Yes."

"So, what you're saying, is a company with American legal ties is involved in a conspiracy involving the kidnapping of American citizens and its allies on foreign soil?"

Leroux smiled. "Yes."

"That's what I thought you said. Then I think your little op has escalated. What assets do we have in the area?"

Leroux motioned at Tong, having already anticipated the question, and a map appeared showing their subjects' last known position and that of his proposed assets, their personnel files appearing on another part of the display. "It just so happens we have a Delta team in Korea instructing their Special Forces."

Morrison's head bobbed as he scanned the personnel files, everyone in the room well acquainted with Bravo Team. "Good. I'll contact Bragg, let them know we need a team to go in. It will have to be a small one though. Mongolia is landlocked between two of our favorite countries, so we can't insert them by sea, HALO them in, or hoof them in."

Leroux pursed his lips. "I see only one option."

"So do I."

Eastern Mongolia

Jack glared at his contact, Major Khurelsukh, ignoring the weapons now pointed at him. "What the hell is this?" he asked in fluent Mongolian. "I thought we had a deal?"

"We did. I said I would fly you out here to find the Americans. I never said where I'd fly you next."

Jack shook his head, sighing. "I think it was implied."

"Not my problem. I have my orders."

"And they are?"

"To watch for those two"—he jabbed a finger at the professors—"and if I come across them, to take them to a classified location."

"And just where is that?"

Khurelsukh smiled. "It's classified." His smile disappeared. "I have no orders with regards to you. We've known each other a long time, Jack. I can leave you here. You can take their car back to Ulaanbaatar, forget this ever happened."

189

Jack stared at him then at the professors. They were nothing to him beyond the mission, but unfortunately for him, the mission was everything, which meant he was about to make the wrong decision. "And if I choose to come along?"

Khurelsukh shrugged. "Then you'll probably share their fate."

"Which is?"

Another shrug. "I don't know, but it can't be good, considering the reward offered for their capture."

"How much?"

"You don't want to know. It just might change your mind about coming."

Jack frowned. "That much, huh?"

"Yup."

"Well, I think I'll come nonetheless, you've got me curious."

Khurelsukh shook his head. "You're a fool, Jack."

"You think I don't know that already?"

United States Army Garrison Humphreys

Pyeongtaek, South Korea

"When you said let's go out for a quick run and burn off some energy, I didn't think you meant ten miles," complained Sergeant Carl "Niner" Sung, a seasoned member of the elite Bravo Team, part of 1st Special Forces Operational Detachment—Delta, commonly known to the public as the Delta Force.

"It ain't worth doing unless it's double digits," rumbled the impossibly muscled Sergeant Leon "Atlas" James.

"Bullshit. I can think of plenty of things that are worth doing that aren't double digits."

"Such as?"

"Making love to a beautiful woman."

Atlas eyed him. "Well, if you think doing that only once is enough, then maybe women aren't your thing."

Sergeant Will "Spock" Lightman laughed. "Somebody call the fire department, you just got burned!"

Niner gave him a look. "Hey, the nineteen-nighties just called, they want their burn back."

Spock flipped him the bird and a grin. "The classics never die."

Atlas interrupted. "So, bringing things back to only wanting to make love to a woman less than ten times in your life, that obviously means you still haven't reached those double digits?"

Niner's fist darted toward Atlas' jaw, the big man catching it effortlessly with an open palm. "You know what I meant."

"It's nothing to be embarrassed about. Lots of people save themselves for marriage."

Niner turned to Command Sergeant Major Burt "Big Dog" Dawson, leading the group. "BD, Atlas is picking on me," he whined. "Can I shoot him?"

Dawson shook his head. "Not until we're stateside. Too much paperwork in Korea."

"Thanks, BD." He grinned at Atlas. "Where do you want it? In the ass?"

"How'd I know you'd go there?"

Everyone roared with laughter, Spock losing his footing and hitting the ground hard, causing a mini pileup. A Humvee rushed onto the scene, a corporal hopping out and running toward the group then coming to a halt in front of Dawson.

"Sergeant Major, a message for you."

Dawson took the paper and read it then turned to the group. "Return to barracks. Niner, Atlas, Spock, be ready to leave ASAP, pack for a business trip. I'll be back to brief you as soon as I can." He climbed into the back of the Humvee leaving the rest of the team picking up those who had tripped over Spock.

"What do you think that's all about?" asked Niner.

Atlas shrugged. "No idea, but it's gotta be more fun than playing teacher."

Operations Center 3, CIA Headquarters

Langley, Virginia

"Did that idiot just say he was going to go with them?"

The Mongolian translator nodded at Leroux. "Yes, sir. He was given the choice between staying and taking the professors' car, or coming with them to this 'classified' location. The classified location has to be the mine. I mean, where else could it be?"

Leroux shook his head. "He doesn't know that, though. He probably thinks he might be able to help them if he goes with them and we track his position." He thought for a moment. "Does he have his watch?"

Child shrugged. "He should."

"Then send him a message."

"If they catch him looking too closely, they might shoot him."

Leroux frowned. "Okay, send it in Morse Code."

"What should it say? Stay?"

"No, he might think it means stay there or stay with them. Just send, 'Don't go.'"

Child tapped at his keyboard. "Done. Now let's just hope he has his watch."

Tong grunted. "And remembers Morse Code."

Eastern Mongolia

Acton held Laura's hand tightly as they sat wedged between Mongolian soldiers, their savior, Jack, sitting across from them, appearing perfectly calm as if nothing untoward had just happened. Acton was dying to ask him what exactly *had* just happened, yet kept his mouth shut, there no knowing what the reaction from the soldiers might be. He doubted they'd shoot him, though a rifle butt to the stomach wasn't exactly appealing either. They'd know soon enough.

Jack suddenly stood and extended his hand toward the man in charge, saying something in Mongolian. There was a brief exchange then the soldier laughed, pointing at the still-open door, the pilot yet to lift off as they powered back up.

Jack stepped over to them. "Did you leave the keys in the car?"

"What?"

"Did you leave the keys in the car? I'm going to need them."

Acton couldn't remember, and patted his pockets, not finding them, and frankly pissed that this coward was about to abandon them. Obviously, the double-cross hadn't extended to him, only them. "I must have left them in the car."

"Okay, thanks." He patted Acton on the shoulder. "Good luck!" Jack hopped out and the helicopter rose into the night sky. As it banked, Acton caught a glimpse of Jack climbing in their rental, the keys obviously still in the ignition as the lights turned on and the car pulled a quick U-turn, their savior heading back to Ulaanbaatar, abandoning them to what fate, he didn't know.

Though he was quite certain neither of them would see dawn.

United States Army Garrison Humphreys

Pyeongtaek, South Korea

Burt "Big Dog" Dawson took a seat in the nondescript briefing room, a panel at the front of the room showing his commanding officer, Colonel Thomas Clancy, and a CIA analyst he had dealt with in the past, Chris Leroux.

"Casual Friday?" asked Clancy with a wry smile.

Dawson glanced down at his jogging gear. "I figured I'd relax while the boss was on the other side of the planet."

Clancy chuckled. He was never one for formalities unless brass bigger than him were in the room. He was a soldier's soldier. Unlike many officers, Dawson was sure Clancy would have been just as comfortable as an NCO as a senior officer. He was a good man, and if it weren't for their differences in station, Dawson could see them being good friends in another life.

"Well, you'll get to stay out of your uniform for a bit longer. We've got a situation that needs your expertise."

"What's up?"

"I'll let Mr. Leroux explain."

Leroux shifted in his seat, still a shy guy, though not the painfully introverted young man he had been only a couple of years ago. "Sergeant Major, good to be working with you again."

"Likewise."

"We have a situation in Mongolia involving Professors Acton and Palmer."

Dawson shook his head. "What else is new? What have they got themselves into this time?"

Leroux grunted. "Well, this time we can definitely lay blame at their feet. Less than forty-eight hours ago, Professor Acton received a text message from a former Mongolian exchange student named Arban Namjiliin. The message indicated he was in trouble, didn't know who to trust, and that he thought someone might kill him."

Dawson sighed. "Well, if that wouldn't get those two charging in to save the day, I don't know what would. Did they at least try outside channels?"

"Yes, Professor Acton sent a secure message to Special Agent Kane, who unfortunately was radio silent at the time. He didn't receive the message until they were almost ready to land."

"This is why civilians shouldn't have access to priority transport."

Clancy chuckled. "At least those two civilians. I still say we should revoke both their passports."

"Agreed."

Leroux continued. "While monitoring Echelon, we discovered that not only was there a lot of activity in Mongolia expressing interest in finding Professor Acton, but that Dean Milton was in trouble at Acton's residence."

Dawson leaned forward, concerned. Milton was a special case, one of his team's biggest regrets. He had given the order, based upon bad intel, to shoot Milton as a terrorist on the President's Termination List. A sanctioned, legal kill. But it had all been a lie, and thankfully because it had been committed in a public restroom, fate had delivered a trauma surgeon into Milton's path only minutes later, saving his life.

Dawson and his team would do anything to protect Milton.

Or avenge him.

"Is he okay?"

"No. He's alive, but was badly beaten and tortured, and there's some question as to whether he'll ever walk again."

Dawson cursed, leaning back in his chair as he glared at the screen. "Please tell me we know who did it."

"I'll do you one better. Sherrie—I mean Agent White, and Lee Fang arrived on the scene, took the assailant into custody, and called for an ambulance."

"Who is he?"

"His name is Willem Du Toit, a known mercenary. He's given up the name of his contact in Mongolia, a Mr. Hendrick Stander, another known mercenary."

"Have you been able to contact the professors?"

"No. We've managed to extract Thomas Granger and Mai Trinh safely, though not without incident. They'll be landing in Seoul soon. We'll arrange for a debriefing."

"Good. And the professors?"

"All we know is that they were heading to what appears to be a strip mine in eastern Mongolia. They were intercepted by one of our agents, but he was double-crossed by his military escort. The Actons are now in Mongolian custody, though we believe they're going to be taken to the mine site."

"And killed?"

"We assume so. Our understanding is that some archaeological discovery was made at the mine site, and they're trying to cover it up."

Dawson's head bobbed. "Because it could kill the operation."

"That's our theory."

"I assume you're Control?"

Leroux nodded. "Yes."

"Good. What's the mission?"

"It's a four-man op. I'd prefer your entire team, but we figure four is the most we can smuggle in without it being noticed."

"The note said to prep for business attire?"

"Yes. You'll be going in as businessmen, there to meet with the government. We've got a private charter arranged that will take you as soon as you're ready. You'll be arriving in the middle of the night, which is unusual, so expect extra scrutiny. We just don't have any time to wait until morning to put you on a commercial flight."

"No problem. We all have our cover IDs with us. Are we expected?"

"We don't believe so."

Dawson's eyebrows rose slightly. "Believe?"

Leroux held up his hands slightly. "Sorry, that's the best reassurance I can offer you. We just don't know. Our intel is very sparse. We're trying to connect to our contact on the ground now. We'll hopefully know more shortly. You should have all the details we know in your secure email, but it's incredibly thin. Communications will be difficult until we get you supplied."

"Through the embassy, I assume?"

"Yes. Hopefully it will be our contact on the ground meeting you. He's as up to date as we are, but he's two hours from your rendezvous. We're hoping he makes it back in time. If he doesn't, we'll have someone else equip you. We've already made hotel reservations for you, so everything should appear legit. The base printers should have business cards and some documents on fake letterhead for you any minute now."

Dawson nodded. "Okay, we'll be ready in fifteen."

"Good luck, Sergeant Major."

Dawson rose. "To all of us."

Eastern Mongolia

Jack had the pedal floored as he tried to shave significant time off the return trip to Ulaanbaatar. Major Khurelsukh hadn't patted him down, in fact, hadn't even confiscated his weapon. It was a clear indication he was of no interest to the major or whoever had hired him to betray him.

He had little doubt this was an oversight on the part of the bigger wallet, and they would be pissed when they found out Khurelsukh had let him go. He had little doubt the major would play the same card he had with him—they hadn't been specific enough.

He chuckled at the balls Khurelsukh had on him.

He tried connecting to Langley again, the satellite uplink giving him nothing but static the last time he tried, making him wonder if the helicopter had activated a jammer.

This time he connected.

"This is Rawhide calling Control, come in, over."

"This is Control, we've got you. I assume you received our message?"

"I did. You better have a damned good reason for having me leave them alone."

"We have assets arriving in a few hours. We need you to rendezvous with them, supply them, then get them to the GPS coordinates the professors were heading to."

He grunted. "Is *that* all? And what makes you think that's where they're heading?"

"The juicy green and black satellite image I'm looking at that shows them on a direct heading to those coordinates. Besides, what were you going to do when you got there? Singlehandedly take out an entire platoon of soldiers, plus whatever private security they have on site?"

He chuckled. He didn't know who Control was today, but he liked him. "Yes."

Control laughed. "I admire your self-confidence."

"As do I, though I'm beginning to think your plan is better. It's going to take me two to three hours to get back and arrange things, then it's a three hour drive back. Do we have that kind of time?"

"We don't believe so. We recommend you try to secure transport that gets you there quicker."

He frowned. "The last time I did that it didn't exactly work out."

"Perhaps try a better class of people to bribe?"

Jack laughed. "I'll take it under advisement. I'll let you know when I reach the city. Contact me if you have any additional information. Right now, I'm doing over a hundred miles per hour on a shitty road in a less than stellar car in the dark. I should be concentrating on my driving."

"Good idea. Control, out."

Jack gripped the wheel tighter, pressing his foot a little harder, the distraction of the conversation having it lifting from the floor slightly. He sighed.

Okay, where the hell am I going to get a helicopter in the middle of the night? And a pilot?

His fingers tapped the steering wheel, then he smiled. Whoever was arriving were likely Special Forces, and there was no way one of them didn't know how to fly a chopper.

One problem solved.

Now he just needed to figure out where to steal one from.

Mine Site, Eastern Mongolia

Arban gently scooped away shovelful after shovelful, dumping each load into a sifter that Elbegdor worked, searching for anything of interest. Lights had been set up to allow them to work through the night, those in charge clearly eager to have everything done before the dayshift arrived.

They were working as fast as they could without compromising the site, but both paused as a helicopter approaching had all those gathered turning. It landed nearby and out of sight from their deep hole, though as the rotors beat at the ground, Arban cursed at the debris blowing into their area. He couldn't discern anything beyond the engines, but as they powered down, he heard something overhead and looked to see the head of security, Stander, staring down into the pit.

"Have they found anything yet?"

Conrad shook his head. "No."

"Why are you humoring them?"

"Why not? If it turns out to be nothing, then we can announce that and continue."

"If not?"

Conrad shrugged. "Well, we'll cross that bridge when we come to it."

Stander shook his head. "I think you're taking a big risk." He pointed at Arban. "Especially with that one."

Conrad stared down at Arban, sending a wave of goosebumps over his body. "Actually, he's proving quite cooperative. I think Elbegdor has converted him to our side."

Stander's eyes probed Arban, who turned away, not trusting he might reveal the truth, instead returning to his work. "You're more trusting than I am."

"Not to worry. If he betrays us again, you have my permission to kill him. Happy?"

"No, but it will have to do. I understand our military contacts have come through for us?" Stander and the others stepped away, out of earshot, leaving Arban to wonder what they were talking about.

Then his shovel hit something, and all that was happening above him was forgotten. He tossed the shovel aside and dug with his spade, gently moving away the dirt and rocks, then gasped as a bone was revealed. He exchanged an excited look with Elbegdor.

"We've found it!" exclaimed his corrupt boss.

"Yes, but what is it we've found?"

Khentii Region, Mongol Empire

1227 AD

It was the deepest hole Mutukan had ever seen. Hundreds had dug it day and night until the scholars among them confirmed it was deep enough to withstand what it would be put through over the years that lay ahead.

The undertaking was ambitious, planned out over days from the moment the spot had been chosen by divine intervention, and as he watched the hand-carved burial bed carrying his beloved master lowered into the hole, to rest upon the stone platform laid at the bottom, his mind turned to the years of service at the man's side. He found his eyes closing as he swayed on his feet, the incantations sung by the monks rhythmic and mesmerizing, enough to put someone to sleep and their ultimate doom should they not be careful.

For the hole was deep, a fall deadly.

A tear rolled down Mutukan's cheek as the ropes slackened, indicating the greatest warrior to have ever lived had reached his final resting place, deep below the surface of the earth, never to be disturbed by anyone again, his peaceful passage into the next life assured.

The monks, finished with their ritual, stepped back, and all those gathered turned, walking away slowly, many sobbing in renewed sorrow.

Mutukan pulled the flat stone he had discovered the day they arrived, now hidden in his robes, and gripped it in his hand, reading the words he had carefully inscribed on it over the many days they had been here. He stepped to the very edge of the hole then held out his arms, the stone gripped in both hands.

And let go.

Breaking his final promise to his master.

In the hope it would ensure his peaceful slumber should something one day go wrong.

Incheon International Airport

Incheon, South Korea

Present Day

Tommy breathed a sigh of relief the moment they stepped into the terminal in South Korea. He hugged Mai. "It's over."

"For us, but not for the professors."

He frowned, guilt washing over him at his selfish thought. "You're right." He looked about. "We need to figure out who to talk to. Jack said to call our parents, but maybe we should call the embassy."

"I think that's a good idea."

Two men in business suits suddenly blocked their path. "Mr. Thomas Granger and Miss Mai Trinh?"

Tommy gulped. "Umm, yes?"

IDs were flashed. "US Federal Agents. I need you to come with us."

"Umm, okay. We were, ahh, actually going to call the embassy."

"Come quickly, there's little time." The man took him by the arm, the other doing the same to Mai, and they were swiftly guided through the crowded terminal, then through a door where they found a small conference room. Four men were sitting on one side of the table. Mai's eyes brightened as she recognized them, and Tommy's heart hammered with excitement, for they were finally, truly, safe.

They were with four members of Bravo Team.

"It's so good to see you all again," gushed Mai as handshakes were exchanged, a bond created during their time together in Vietnam where she had helped save Niner's life and that of the rest of the team. And a heavy price paid by never being able to go home. "Why are you here?" she asked as they all sat back down.

Dawson took the lead. "This will be a very quick meeting, I'm afraid. We're heading to Mongolia to retrieve the professors, so we need to know everything you know."

Tommy's stomach flipped. "Does that mean they've been captured?"

"Yes. As far as we can tell, they've been taken into custody by corrupt Mongolian military, and are being taken to a mine site located at the GPS coordinates you found."

Tommy frowned. "Well, it sounds like you know everything we do then."

"Do you have the data you retrieved off Mr. Arban Namjiliin's computer?"

Tommy shook his head. "No, it was all on my laptop. The Internet connection was so slow, I never had time to upload anything into the cloud."

"Where's your laptop?"

"In my hotel room, I think." He shook his head. "Actually, that guy who tried to kidnap us put it in a bag. They had it with them when Jack rescued us." He cursed. "They probably have his home computer too. That means nobody has a copy of those photos anymore."

Dawson leaned forward. "What exactly do the photos show?"

"A skeletal hand, some carved wood. Nothing much, but it was enough to get her excited." He jerked a thumb toward Mai.

Mai smiled. "I'm an archaeologist by training. Of course I'm going to get excited by something found deep underground in the middle of nowhere."

Dawson waved a hand, cutting off what Tommy was certain would be a detailed explanation. "Okay, we'll let the scientists worry about the science. Our job is to rescue the hostages if we can reach them in time. Is there anything helpful you can tell us that might achieve that?"

Tommy shrugged. "I'm sorry, I can't think of anything. We were in our hotel room almost the entire time. Beyond the GPS coordinates— oh, wait! Before I forget! The Mongolians arrested two innocent people at the airport, thinking they were us. Is there anything you can do to help them?"

Dawson frowned. "I'll let Control know, and they'll see what they can do." He rose, followed by the rest of the room. "There's a flight waiting to take you stateside. The men outside will see that you're on it."

Tommy took Mai's hand. "We'd rather wait to make sure the professors are okay."

Dawson regarded them. "Can you think of any way that you'd be able to help us by being here?"

Tommy stared at him blankly as he struggled to think of something, anything, that wouldn't make his statement sound as stupid as it was. "Umm, no? But just because I can't think of anything now, doesn't mean I won't later."

Dawson chuckled. "I like you, kid. Get on the plane. If you're needed, or you think of anything, call Control. You've dealt with him before. Chris Leroux."

Tommy nodded. "Yeah, I know him."

"Good. Then you know anything you say he'll take seriously. Get on the flight, get home, so that when we do rescue the professors, they have one less thing to worry about, okay?"

Mai looked up at Tommy. "He's right. Let's just get home and out of the way."

Tommy agreed. "Fine, but try to do something about those people who were arrested. They don't deserve to be in a jail cell because of us."

Dawson ushered them out the door. "I will."

Mine Site, Eastern Mongolia

Acton stared out one of the small windows of the Mil Mi-24 Hind helicopter as it banked to land at what was obviously a strip mine, the massive open pit lost in the darkness, one area intensely lit, and if he didn't know better, a portion of it staked off as if there was an archaeological dig underway.

They landed, the massive rotors powering down as the doors were thrown open and the soldiers poured out, two of them hauling him and Laura to their feet and shoving them outside. Acton hit the ground hard, cursing at the men as he turned his attention to Laura who had managed to maintain her footing. He struggled to his feet, his hands still cuffed behind him, then surveyed their new surroundings.

It was definitely a mine, massive equipment everywhere, though beyond this small area, the active mine itself didn't appear to be running, which he found sort of surprising, as he would have thought the operation would run in shifts, 24 hours a day. He stared toward the staked site but couldn't see it, a large hole, freshly dug if the dirt piled beside it was any indication, all that was visible. The soldiers had spread out, creating a perimeter, the major in charge already talking to several civilians, all but one Caucasian.

"Are you okay?"

He nodded at Laura. "You?"

"Yeah. What do you think is going on?"

He shook his head. "I don't know. This is obviously where they were taking the core samples, so that means they're looking to expand the operation."

She stared at the massive open pit in the distance. "Looks pretty big to me already."

"Me too. Did you see that staked out area when we flew by?"

"Yes. But it can't be because of what was in that photo, could it? I mean, if they were going to properly excavate, why all the shooting?"

He shrugged. "Your guess is as good as mine." He noticed the group of civilians walk toward them. "Okay, maybe we're about to find out what's going on."

"Or we're about to get shot."

Acton grunted. "Well, let's ask lots of questions before they do that. If I die, I want to know why."

She pressed against him, staring up at him. "If we die, I just want you to know that I love you."

"Only *if?*"

She smiled, whacking him gently with a twist of her shoulders. "You know what I mean."

"I love you too." He leaned down and gave her a kiss.

"Aww, isn't that touching."

Acton glared at the man with a South African accent, a man he recognized as part of the second group to have arrived at Arban's house. "It's called love. You should try it sometime. Maybe you wouldn't be such a prick."

The man chuckled. "You know, Professor Acton, in another life, you and I might have been friends."

Acton grunted. "I doubt it." He looked at the group. "Now, who's in charge here. Surely it can't be this hired gun."

A man stepped forward. Caucasian, mid-forties, tidy haircut and expensive though business-casual clothes. "I am."

"And you are?"

"His name is none of your business," interrupted the South African.

The man in charge glanced at him, shaking his head. "I hardly think it matters anymore, do you, Stander? I mean, if we're killing them, then they take the names to their grave. And if we aren't, then what the hell was the point of all this?"

Acton's stomach churned at the words. Their lives were forfeit, but there was still hope. Jack was still out there. He knew where they were going, was almost definitely CIA, which meant Kane knew they were in trouble. That all added up to a hell of a lot of hope with the friends they had acquired over the years. Yet it wasn't like they were exactly the next town over. They would need time to get here, and that meant he had to delay things.

"If you're going to kill us, can you at least tell us why, Mister...?"

"Conrad. I'm the Vice President of Operations at FirstPrime Mining, here to oversee the expansion of this mine."

"And just what is it you mine here?"

"The most important materials of the modern economy. Tell me, Professor, what do you think that is?"

Acton didn't have to think hard. The man had said 'modern,' and they were willing to kill to keep it running. And he had heard of FirstPrime. They had operations back home. American companies didn't kill over copper or nickel, even gold or diamonds. Not today. But with what was happening in the world today, there was something he could see causing greed to replace sense. "Rare earth elements."

Conrad clapped as he laughed, exchanging jovial looks with the others who remained stone-faced. "Give the man a cigar! Exactly right, Professor."

"But why kill?" asked Laura. "It's just a mine."

"Just a mine! Do you realize how important a resource this is? What we've found here is massive. This deposit could help shift the balance away from China. Do you realize they provide eighty percent of the entire global market? That means, on a whim, they can shut off our supplies, and cripple our hi-tech economy in a matter of months. That means no new cellphones, computers, medical equipment, televisions. And it's not just consumer goods. Do you realize how dependent our military is on these materials?

"And look at the state of our relations with China right now. How long before they take that step? They could do it tomorrow if the wrong thing is said or done. But this mine, this ground we're standing on right here, right now, can change all that. Once at full capacity, we could reduce the global dependence on Chinese supplied product dramatically, to the point that if they shut off their supplies, we could fill a significant chunk of the demand and minimize the risk to our economy."

Acton hated when the villain was right, but in this case, Conrad was. He had read the articles. And with each passing year, as China's economy grew stronger, as its technological capabilities improved, and as its military might grew, especially its blue water navy capabilities, they would overtake the United States and become the preeminent superpower on the planet. And with the grip it held on things such as rare earth elements, desperately needed by the modern way of life Western civilization demanded, they could shut off our access to it and there would be nothing we could do beyond complain to a dictator-dominated United Nations.

He stared at Conrad. "I agree with every word you just said."

Conrad's eyebrows shot up. "You do?"

"Of course. I'm an educated man, I've read the articles. This mine is essential to the future of our economy. I agree. And if our silence is what you need to keep this operation going, then you have my word that you'll have it."

Conrad chuckled. "Professor Acton, do you take me for a fool?"

Acton gave a wry smile. "I was hoping you were."

Stander laughed, the others joining in. "I knew I liked him."

Conrad stepped closer, the diminutive man staring up at Acton. "Professor, I obviously can't take your word for it, and that *is* unfortunate."

218

Acton had to agree. "Can you tell me something, though?"

Conrad stepped back, shrugging. "Why not? The condemned man is entitled to a final request."

"What did you do to Arban? Did you kill him?"

Conrad shook his head, extending his arm toward the pit where Acton had spotted the staked-out area. "No. Your friend Arban has joined our side. In fact, he's over there, excavating our little unfortunate discovery."

Acton's eyes narrowed. "Why? If you're willing to kill people, then why bother preserving the find?"

"Because if it turns out to be nothing, then we can continue operations, and if word managed to spread, we can claim we followed proper procedure, found it was nothing, and continued on."

"And if it does prove to be something?" asked Laura.

"No problem. We move it somewhere else, then have it 'discovered' there, with no one the wiser."

Acton resisted the urge to exchange what he was certain would have been an all too revealing glance with Laura. Unless these morons exactly matched the soil types, content, and much more, any archaeologist worth his salt would determine very quickly the discovery had been transplanted. Though they might have difficulty proving exactly where it had been moved from, as he doubted there were a lot of soil samples on record for this area to compare to, they wouldn't fool anyone in the end.

But they would never have the discovery traced back to them.

Maybe they're not morons.

A sudden thought occurred to him. "Can I make one more request?"

"What's that?"

"Let us help with the excavation."

Conrad's eyes narrowed. "And why would I let you do that?"

"Because with two more sets of professional hands, the job will get done that much faster."

Conrad regarded him for a moment. "Why do I think you're up to something?"

Acton shrugged. "Your distrusting nature?" He gestured at the soldiers and private security. "It's not exactly like we can go anywhere now, is it?"

Conrad pursed his lips and Stander stepped forward.

"Sir, you're not actually—"

Conrad cut him off with a raised hand. "We agreed to a proper excavation to keep our Mongolian friends happy. We need their cooperation. And the sooner it gets done, the sooner we can put this behind us. Whether you shoot them now or a few hours from now makes no difference, does it?"

Stander glared at Acton. "No, assuming nothing goes wrong. Those kids at the hotel had outside help and three of my men are dead. He's still out there somewhere. And those kids knew where this mine was. They didn't know it was a mine, but somehow they had the GPS coordinates for this place."

Conrad dismissed his concerns. "He's one man. The Americans don't exactly have a presence here."

"No, but she's rich. I think he's private security."

Conrad regarded Stander. "Even so, if he had more men with him, would he have taken all four of you on alone?"

Stander frowned. "No, I suppose not."

"Then there you go. CIA or private, it doesn't matter. He's one man. If he comes here, we kill him too." Conrad pointed at Acton and Laura. "Get them out of those cuffs and into the hole. I want that excavation completed before dawn."

Acton suppressed the smile that so desperately wanted to escape.

He had just bought them hours.

Come on, Jack, work your magic!

En route to Mongolia

Dawson leaned back in the ridiculously comfortable seat of the charter jet, trying to catch a little shuteye before they arrived. The distinctive snap of traditional playing cards to his right was a comfort, Spock always carrying an old deck with him wherever he went so he could kill time playing solitaire.

"You know, you can play that on your phone."

Dawson opened his eyes to see Niner leaning over Spock's seat from behind.

Spock cocked an eyebrow. "And what would the point of that be?"

Niner shrugged. "You wouldn't look like such a Luddite?"

Spock continued to play. "And what's so bad about shunning technology every once in a while?"

Niner spun his phone on the tip of his finger. "I could never live without my girl."

Atlas returned from the bathroom waving his hand. "I highly recommend nobody go back there for a few days." He grabbed Niner's spinning phone. "And if this is your girlfriend, maybe that's why you don't want to make love to a beautiful woman more than ten times in your life."

Niner snatched the phone back and gave it a gentle pet. "You don't listen to him, Siri, you know you're my girl."

Atlas dropped in a seat across from Spock. "You know, I was reading about these rare earth elements. They're in everything now! And China controls most of it. They could hurt us badly if they wanted to."

Dawson raised his seat, sleep apparently not on the agenda. "Which is probably why somebody is willing to kidnap or worse, kill, to keep their mine going. The companies and countries that can position themselves to pick up the slack should the Chinese make a move, will make a killing."

Niner shook his head. "I still can't believe people are actually killing because of this. An American company! I hope the Feds are taking action."

"Last update from Control says the Feds are going to be raiding their offices the moment we give the all-clear. They don't want to risk the hostages."

"Good. Shut the mothers down."

Atlas grunted. "That's never going to happen. A company that big? They'll just fire a few executives, pay some fines, then continue on as if nothing ever happened. That's the thing about corporations. They can get away with pretty much anything, because most of them aren't just one person. They're hundreds, thousands, tens of thousands. They just designate a fall guy, then continue on as if nothing happened. They'll claim whoever is running things in Mongolia was acting on his own, that they had no idea what he was doing, and nobody will be able to prove otherwise, unless some idiot sent an email. I'll bet a month of Niner's salary that in the end, nobody even sees the inside of a prison cell."

Niner checked that his wallet was still in his pocket. "While I appreciate your willingness to risk my money, I hate to think our system is that broken that you could be right."

Atlas shook his head. "Look at the financial crisis! We bailed out those banks and a year later they're bonusing out over a hundred and fifty million to the executives that caused the damned crisis. They just don't care."

Spock's eyebrow shot up. "So, all corporations are evil?"

Atlas wagged a finger at him. "Hey, I never said that. I think most are good, especially the small to mid-size ones. They're hard-working people trying to make a living. But when they get so big that everyone is just a number, and the almighty dollar becomes king rather than doing what's morally right? Then you start to have problems. Not with them all, but with some.

"And keep in mind, these companies can be massive. If you've got a thousand or ten thousand people working for you, how the hell do you keep track of what they're doing? I mean, yes, they're all in your computer, so you know where they're supposed to be and what their next paycheck is going to be, but when you're that big, the guy at the top has to delegate. And just because you're an employee, an executive, doesn't mean you're a good guy. Criminals have jobs too. I'm willing to bet that the head office back in Seattle has no clue what their guy is up to in Mongolia. He probably sends them status reports saying everything is hunky-dory, and as long as the profits keep rolling in, they ignore the entire operation. It's not like he's going to add an addendum to his 'Good morning, Seattle' email that says, oh, by the way, I executed six people last night because they found out we broke some local law."

Dawson regarded him. "I'm guessing you're right. And that means we could have somebody completely off his rocker running the operation. The one they arrested in Maryland at the professors' house has quite the record, and has been associated with some pretty nasty guys over the years. They won't hesitate to shoot to kill if they're like him."

Niner sat back in his seat. "I saw the photos of what was done to Dean Milton. That deserves a bullet to the head as far as I'm concerned."

Dawson nodded. "Agreed."

Atlas eyed him. "So, what you're saying is…"

"What I'm saying is that when we arrive, assume everyone wants to kill you, and don't hesitate to shoot to kill."

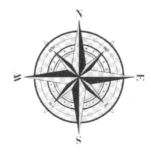

Mine Site, Eastern Mongolia

Acton rubbed his wrists, thankful to be rid of the cuffs the Mongolian soldiers had put on them when they had been captured. He took Laura's hand and walked down the earthen ramp and into the large hole dug earlier.

Arban spotted them and smiled.

Then frowned.

"Professor Acton? They got you too?"

Acton shrugged as he shook Arban's hand. "It would appear so." He turned to Laura. "I don't think you've met my wife. Arban Namjiliin, may I present Professor Laura Palmer."

Laura shook the young man's hand. "A pleasure."

"I wish it were under better circumstances." Arban sighed. "I'm so sorry I got you mixed up in this."

Acton shook his head. "No, don't apologize. This isn't your fault." He glanced up at their captors, standing at the edge of the hole. "It's their fault."

"Yes, but now we're all going to die."

Acton smiled slightly. "Never give up hope, my friend."

Arban grunted, jerking a thumb at another man on his hands and knees. "You sound like him."

"And he is?"

"My corrupt boss, and the reason we're all here. Bataar Elbegdor."

Acton frowned. "I see." He gestured toward the staked off area. "You obviously remember your training."

Arban grinned. "How could I forget? I had the best teacher."

Laura patted Acton's shoulder. "He is that, isn't he?"

Acton stepped toward the dig. "So, what have you found?"

"A body only minutes ago. I hate to say this, but you couldn't have arrived at a better time."

Acton grunted. "I just wish I had arrived with a Delta platoon."

Arban eyed him. "What's that?"

"Wishful thinking." Acton pointed at the excavation. "Continue."

"We've reached the level the core sample indicated the void with the skeletal hand should be. We've just begun excavating the rest of the skeleton."

"Anything significant yet?"

"No, like I said, we reached it only minutes before you arrived." He jutted his chin toward those standing watch. "They don't like us doing anything without someone watching."

Acton looked up and spotted Stander staring at him. The man leaned closer, his hands on one knee.

"Remember, Professor, if you try anything, I'll kill your wife first and let you watch."

Khentii Region, Mongol Empire

1227 AD

"Kill them all."

The general nodded, his face grim, knowing full well that this was but the first of several orders to come that would be unpleasant.

Yet completely necessary.

Mutukan's chest ached as the order was barked, the elite personal guard of a thousand mounted men, all lined up before them, turning to execute the orders they likely suspected were coming, though probably had hoped weren't.

They spread out in a long line across the open grounds they had discovered weeks before. The Khan's resting place was deep under it now, their leader resting peacefully under a river diverted from several hundred paces away. The former riverbed had been filled in with the dirt dug from the new, with thousands of trees now planted overtop it.

Unless someone was intimately familiar with the area, no one would know the river had been shifted.

And no one would think to look under flowing water for the body of Genghis Khan should they wish to desecrate his grave and disturb his slumber.

He watched as the tens of thousands of workers employed over the past weeks were herded out of the area. There could be no evidence left behind that so many had been here. All of their belongings had already been burnt, the ashes tossed into the river, the ground replanted.

And in the next valley, where the river merged with another, forming an even mightier flow to the ocean, those that had served their Khan would be sacrificed to preserve the secret, their bodies tossed into the river to be carried out to sea, leaving no mass grave to be found.

For no one could know the location of the tomb of Genghis Khan.

Ulaanbaatar, Mongolia

Present Day

Jack smiled at the irony of it. Beyond the fence sat nearly a dozen beautiful helicopters, but one fenced off area had his preferred choice. A custom-painted job promoting the company that owned it. FirstPrime Mining. There were two helipads in the closed-off area, one vacant. He wasn't certain if they had one chopper, or if the second were elsewhere, perhaps at the mine, but he didn't care. All that mattered was that this one was here, and that it stayed here until the Delta team arrived.

And he needed to know if it was functional.

He cut the fence, carefully listening for any security—especially canine—then made for the helicopter at a crouch. He opened the door, the fact it was unlocked giving him hope for the next check—did the helicopter need a key to start? Many didn't, and those that did often had the key left inside.

After all, only a helicopter pilot could steal a helicopter.

He checked the cockpit controls, finding no evidence of a key needed, then flipped several switches, his knowledge basic. The helicopter powered up its electronics and he confirmed it was fully fueled.

Now we've got our ride.

He powered down, then stealthily returned to the professors' rental, his two hours of driving giving him plenty of time to figure out everything that needed to be done to expedite their rescue. He started the engine and headed for the embassy as he checked his watch. The team was due to arrive shortly, and they'd be coming in with nothing but civilian accouterments.

Now to get some weapons of war.

Operations Center 3, CIA Headquarters
Langley, Virginia

Leroux frowned as he stared at the satellite image of the mine site, the Mil Mi-24 Hind gunship still on the ground, its rotors at rest.

They're not going anywhere anytime soon.

"That's a lot of guns on site," said Child. "Our guys are going to be heavily outnumbered."

Tong agreed. "Not to mention they'll be engaging Mongolian military. This has international incident written all over it."

Leroux sat in his chair, folding his arms as he sought a solution while counting far too many green dots on the screen, each representing an armed hostile.

"What's that?" asked Child, zooming in on an area. Four people were in what appeared to be a hole. "Are they digging?"

Leroux rose, approaching the display. "They look like they're on their hands and knees." He squinted. "Increase the contrast." He pointed at what appeared to be lines. "What are those?"

Child manipulated the image and a series of squares appeared.

Leroux whistled. "Does that look like an archaeological dig to anyone else?"

Tong nodded. "Definitely. Could two of those be the professors?"

"Bring up the photo from the last flyby."

Child tapped his keyboard, bringing up an image from a couple of hours ago, then zoomed in on the same area.

Leroux smiled. "Same grid, but only two people." He slapped his hands together. "I think they convinced them to let them work on whatever the hell that is. And you know what that means."

Tong smiled. "They just bought us the time we need."

Genghis Khan International Airport

Ulaanbaatar, Mongolia

Customs had hassled them a little more than usual, a last-minute charter flight arriving in the middle of the night unusual for the Mongolians. But they had nothing to hide.

On the surface.

Their luggage were all carry-ons containing nothing but clothing and normal items businessmen carried on quick trips. No secret compartments, no deodorant sticks hiding miniaturized radios.

Nothing whatsoever to accidentally find.

And that appeared to frustrate the guards.

Their paperwork was good, their covers well-traveled and thoroughly documented, and the base printers had done top-notch jobs on their business cards, Langley providing a previously created package of fake paperwork to fill their briefcases. To all outward appearances, they were businessmen coming to meet with the embassy liaison, then with the local government about improving the poor communications infrastructure.

"No samples?"

Dawson stared at the customs official. "Excuse me?"

"Why no samples? You not bring samples to show our government?"

Dawson smiled. "Oh, sorry, I'm so tired, I didn't hear you. They were already sent a couple of weeks ago." He winked. "That's why we got the meeting."

The guard's mouth opened in understanding as his head bobbed. "Were they cellphones?"

Dawson nodded.

"Nice?"

"Nothing but the best." He leaned forward and handed the man his business card, lowering his voice. "I'll tell you what. In one week, email me your address and I'll hook you up. Just tell me how many of your boys here would like some state-of-the-art hardware."

The man's eyes bulged and he took the card, quickly stuffing it in his pocket. He waved toward the doors. "You can go. Welcome to Mongolia."

Dawson bowed his head and made for the door with the others. Niner came up beside him.

"You know he's going to ask for a couple of hundred phones."

Dawson shrugged. "Hey, depending on how much Langley wants to keep this cover company legit, they might just send them."

Niner laughed. "Good thing you didn't promise them tanks."

They exited the terminal, the crisp nighttime air greeting them, along with a Caucasian man standing beside an idling SUV, sporting a smile. "Hiya, boys."

Dawson extended a hand. "Jack, I presume?"

"Pleasure to meet you boys from corporate. Now, load your luggage in the back, and I'll get you to your hotel."

Dawson played along with the cover. There were definitely eyes in the area, and Jack apparently wasn't willing to risk tipping anyone off by letting anything slip. Within minutes, they were in the city, the traffic sparse, the tinted windows providing them with privacy.

"I've got gifts in the back."

Niner and Atlas retrieved four large duffel bags.

"Body armor, MP5s, Glocks, ammo, flashbangs, the works. You gotta love America's desire to be able to wage covert wars in every country in the world."

Dawson chuckled. "God bless the United States of America, and the fine weaponry freedom provides." He inspected a Glock handed forward by Spock. "So, what's the latest?"

"The professors are at the mine site as we suspected. According to Langley, they appear to be working in some archaeological dig with two other people."

Niner leaned forward between the seats. "Are you serious? They actually convinced the bad guys to put them to work?"

Dawson grunted. "Whatever the reason, it probably saved their lives. If I know the professors, they did this on purpose to buy time." He looked at Jack. "Speaking of, my understanding is that this mine is several hours drive from here. I assume you got us something faster." He tipped his head forward slightly. "Something *not* Mongolian military."

Jack snorted. "Jeez, you screw up just one time and nobody ever lets you forget it." He made a turn. "I'll have you know, I have secured us a nice little ride that will get us there in a third of the time, if not better." He glanced at Dawson. "Assuming one of you knows how to fly a helicopter."

Dawson smiled. "Pilots are one thing we're not short of."

"Fantastic." Jack made another turn. "Now let's just hope nobody already flew away with it."

"Excuse me?"

Jack gave a toothy smile. "Nothing!"

Mine Site, Eastern Mongolia

Acton sat on his haunches, staring at what they had uncovered over the past several hours. It was a complete skeleton less one hand, with no evidence of scavengers having torn apart the carcass of an abandoned body.

This man had been buried.

And with honors.

His clothing and armor were still partially intact, his weapons had been laid out with purpose at his sides, along with a substantial amount of gold coins, likely meant to ease his transition into the next life.

It was an amazing find, of definite archaeological significance.

If the laws were obeyed, it was enough to bring the operation to a halt, and perhaps even enough to halt it permanently, though he doubted that. A substantial hole had been dug here, and there was no evidence that anything else had been located. This was not a graveyard, nor a village.

It was a lone grave, literally in the middle of nowhere.

"We can move this."

Acton regarded Elbegdor, Arban's corrupt boss, who had performed admirably over the past several hours, the man genuinely interested in preserving what they had found. "I assume you mean move it so that it can be 'found' somewhere else?"

Elbegdor nodded. "I'm happy you have a grasp of the situation, Professor Acton. I figured you would."

"So, now that we've discovered what it is, and you've decided it can be moved, what happens to us?"

"I'm afraid that's out of my control."

Acton eyed Elbegdor. "I had a feeling you were going to say that. And Arban? What about him?"

Elbegdor sighed, glancing at the young man. "I'm afraid with your arrival, it complicates things."

Acton shook his head. "No, it doesn't. Kill us, but let him live. He's done nothing wrong."

Elbegdor stared at Acton. "You really mean that, don't you? You'd really trade your lives for his?"

"In a heartbeat."

"I believe you would." Elbegdor exhaled loudly. "Unfortunately, there's no choice to be made here. If you hadn't arrived, then I think I could have convinced those above to spare his life. After all, what we have found can be moved, and the threat of harming his wife would have kept him in line. But with you two, you can't be allowed to leave. You know too much, and are too well-respected. You'll leave here and tell the world, and it will cause us too many problems."

"And if we promised we wouldn't?"

Elbegdor smiled. "While *I* might believe you, there is no possible way they will." He nodded toward their observers above. "I'm afraid your fate is sealed, and because of it, my poor friend's here as well. Too many people know you came here because of a message he sent. They'll come looking for you, find him, and he'll feel compelled to tell the truth." He frowned. "There's simply too much to lose."

Arban threw a stone across the hole. "So, if I hadn't texted Professor Acton, everyone would still be alive."

Elbegdor nodded. "I'm afraid so."

"What's this?"

Everyone turned to Laura, who had continued working, ignoring their impending doom.

"What?" asked Acton as he joined her on the other side of the body. His eyes narrowed at the piece of stone, perhaps the size of an iPad, lying beside the body. "Is that writing?"

"Looks like it." She took a brush and removed as much of the dirt as she could. "It looks like there should be a second half. Be careful where you step."

Arban raised his hand. "Found it!" He pointed at a piece of stone sticking up from out of the dirt.

Acton smiled. "Go ahead, you know what to do."

Arban grinned then grabbed his spade, carefully excavating around the stone, its entire surface soon revealed, more writing clearly visible.

Acton lifted the first piece from the ground, Arban doing the same with his. Acton took them both and pressed them together.

"What does it say?" asked Arban as he repositioned for a better view.

Acton shook his head. "No idea. It's in Mongolian."

Elbegdor leaned forward. "That's Ancient Mongolian. I can read it." He shone a flashlight on the broken tablet then gasped.

"What does it say?" asked Laura, as excited as Acton was.

"It says, 'Here lies the body of the great Temüjin, lost in glorious battle. May he rule in the next life as he did in this.'"

Acton fell back onto the ground, his heart slamming as his jaw dropped.

Temüjin.

He stared at the body of the greatest warrior, the greatest murderer, of all time, a chill rushing over him at what it meant. It was one of the greatest finds in history, and the Mongolian government, the Mongolian people, would never stand for it to be disturbed.

Not for all the money in the world.

This mine was finished.

If only someone knew.

Conrad shouted from above. "What is it? Have you found something?"

Elbegdor held up the tablet. "It's him!"

"Who?"

"Genghis Khan!"

En route to Mine Site, Eastern Mongolia

Dawson adjusted his mike as Leroux brought them up to date.

"The Hind is still on the ground with no sign of leaving. You've got what looks like platoon strength on the ground—Mongolian regulars. There are at least another half-dozen that were already there. We're guessing they are part of the private security working the mine. If they're anything like the guy we have sitting in one of our interrogation rooms, they're the ones you have to worry about."

Dawson rolled his eyes at the others. "So, what you're saying is that we're up against eighteen armed men."

"At least."

"Uh-huh. Okay, what are our ROEs? Can we engage the Mongolians directly?"

"Negative, not unless they shoot first."

No surprise there.

"And the private security?"

"Open season."

"Understood." He turned to Jack. "ETA?"

"Ten minutes."

"Okay, land short. I don't want them hearing us coming. We'll hoof it in the rest of the way."

Jack frowned. "If I'd known I was going for a jog, I would have worn more appropriate shoes."

Dawson chuckled. "You'll *wish* you were going for a jog."

Mine Site, Eastern Mongolia

Conrad ran down the ramp with Stander then rushed over to the group gathered around the skeleton. "What did you say?" he asked, his tone hushed.

Elbegdor responded for the group, not bothering with the hushed tone. "I said it's Genghis Khan."

Conrad's eyes widened. "Keep your damned voice down! Do you realize what would happen if those soldiers found out? Half of them are probably shamanists and would think we just desecrated the grave of one of their gods."

Acton held his tongue for the man was right. Genghis Khan was a shamanist in his day, and much of Mongolia still held those beliefs. And those who practiced shamanism now believed Genghis Khan was a shaman, and was revered like no other. There was no telling what would happen if the soldiers above knew what was going on.

"You have to shut down this section of the mine," said Elbegdor.

Conrad glared at him. "Are you kidding me? That is precisely why you are *not* here. I pay you and your friends good money to look the other way just in case we find something like this."

Elbegdor shook his head. "Not like this!" He jabbed a finger at the uncovered tomb. "This is Genghis Khan! The greatest Mongol to have ever lived. He is revered by millions, and this has now become the most significant archaeological find in the entire country, if not the entire continent. This cannot be just ignored. I must report this to my superiors."

Stander gripped his weapon. "I don't think I can allow that."

Conrad held up a hand. "Now, let's everybody calm down. Elbegdor, you'll go to jail along with the rest of us. You know that, don't you?"

Elbegdor shook his head. "I don't care. I'd happily face the firing squad if it meant preserving the tomb of Genghis Khan."

Stander sneered. "If a firing squad is what you want, I can provide one." He drew his weapon.

Acton finally decided he had to say something. "Okay, everyone just calm down a minute. Mr. Elbegdor, if this were discovered legitimately, what would happen?"

"What do you mean?"

"I mean, would it stay here? Would you build around it, or would you move it?"

Elbegdor sighed. "I don't know. As a scientist, I would say we preserve it intact and in place, but with where it is, it's impractical. Most likely, the powers that be would insist it be moved to Ulaanbaatar where it could be properly secured. But there is more to it than that."

"What?" asked Laura. "You mean his wishes?"

"Exactly. It was the Khan's wish that he be buried in accordance with his people's traditions, in an unmarked grave where his corporeal body could be forgotten. Now that it has been found, what do we do to satisfy his wishes?"

Stander shook his head. "Who gives a shit? He's been dead what, a thousand years? Who cares what his wishes were?"

Acton sighed. "Oh, I don't know, about three million Mongolians? Khan is like a god to many of the people in this country. Ignoring a god's wishes isn't an option. We have to take that into account."

Stander stared at the body. "Why don't we just rebury it?"

Conrad wagged a finger. "No, that's not an option. This expansion will be opened on schedule." He jabbed a finger at the tomb. "That thing must be out of here before dawn."

Elbegdor shook his head. 'That's impossible. Even if we agree it has to be moved, it will take time to properly excavate it."

"How long?"

"Days for sure, more likely weeks."

Conrad's head shook vehemently. "Out of the question. It's moving in the next two hours."

"I can't allow that."

"You have no choice in the matter."

Stander growled. "I'll handle this!" He stormed up the dirt ramp built earlier by the excavator as everyone stared after him, the mercenary disappearing after cresting the edge. An engine roared to life and Acton gasped as a massive loader appeared, its scoop raised, Stander behind the controls as he guided it down the ramp.

"No!" cried Acton as he rushed foolishly toward it, Laura grabbing him by the arm and hauling him back. Elbegdor cried out, racing toward the ramp.

"Stop! What are you doing? Stop!" He turned to Conrad. "Make him stop, please! I'll do whatever you want!"

Conrad shrugged as he stepped out of the way of the approaching vehicle. "I think this will resolve things quite expediently."

Elbegdor stared at the others desperately, then did something unexpected.

He dropped to his knees then lay in front of the loader. Stander laughed, showing no signs of slowing down.

"No!" Arban rushed forward and grabbed Elbegdor by the belt and hauled him out of the way as Stander rolled over the patch of dirt that Elbegdor had occupied moments before. Acton grabbed Laura by the hand and they rushed out of the way as Stander spun the vehicle 90 degrees, lowering the bucket to ground level, then advanced. Acton reached for a non-existent weapon on his hip, then turned to see if Conrad had one.

He didn't.

He stared up at the soldiers, all armed, staring into the pit, clearly ignorant as to what was about to happen. Acton grabbed Arban and pointed at the soldiers above. "Tell them what's happening!"

"What?"

"Tell them!"

Arban's eyes widened at what was being asked of him. He turned and cupped his hands around his mouth to be heard over the roar of the engine behind him, and yelled.

Major Khurelsukh's eyes shot wide as he heard the words hollered from the hole.

"He's going to destroy the tomb of Genghis Khan!"

He rushed to the edge, staring down as the loader rolled forward toward what was supposed to be a trivial archaeological find. And his mouth went dry. If this were indeed the tomb of the great shaman, then his career would be over and he'd be found dead in the mountains somewhere, tossed from his helicopter, the official report listing him as missing, presumed dead after an accident.

"Sir? Is it true?"

Khurelsukh ignored his second in command, Lieutenant Jalair, instead contemplating his options. None were good.

"Sir! We have to stop them! If there's even a chance!"

Khurelsukh spun at him. "No! Follow my orders!"

"But it's the great Khan!"

"One more word and I'll have you up on charges!"

Jalair's eyes were wide, his head shaking, the young man clearly panicking. "No! They must be stopped."

Khurelsukh reached for his sidearm but it was too late. Jalair raised his AK-47 and fired. Khurelsukh felt each round slam into his chest and abdomen, and before he hit the ground, dead, chaos erupted.

Gunfire raged overhead as Stander shoved the scoop into the carefully uncovered tomb. Acton stared helplessly as the massive piece of machinery tore into the dirt before it finally came to a halt, the gaping maw of the beast now containing the entire excavation.

Remarkably intact.

There might still be hope.

Laura grabbed his arm and pulled him toward the wall of the hole nearest the helicopter, as gunfire rained down from above, pinging off the yellow-painted metal, the soldiers finally attempting to stop Stander. Acton glanced over his shoulder as he slammed into the dirt wall, covering Laura as ricochets rocketed off the thick metal, hammering into the dirt walls surrounding it, small explosions of earth erupting around them as near misses continued to threaten them. Stander was nowhere to be seen, but the distinct sound of a pistol joining the mix suggested he was alive and well and fighting back.

Something hit the dirt hard behind him and his head swiveled to see what it was. A Mongolian soldier. Another dropped by his side and Acton realized what was going on.

These soldiers were barely trained.

Stander's men were well-seasoned mercenaries. Though outnumbered, they far outclassed those they were against. He had to even the odds. He dropped to a crouch and rushed over to the closest body, grabbing the AK-47 still gripped in the soldier's hands. He found two spare magazines on the man's belt and stuffed them in his pocket.

Laura bolted past him, grabbing the AK off the second soldier, retrieving a single extra mag. He held a finger to his lips, signaling for silence as he scanned the area for cover from which to fire.

And found nothing but the loader.

But where were Arban and Elbegdor? If he couldn't see them, then perhaps they had found the exact cover they needed to fight back.

Dawson cursed and their hoofing turned into a sprint as he activated his comm. "Control, Zero-One. What the hell is going on, over?"

"Zero-One, it looks like all hell's breaking loose. ETA?"

"You tell me."

"If you maintain your pace, you should be in range inside of two minutes. Be advised, it appears the Mongolian regulars have engaged the private security."

Dawson lengthened his stride. "Who's winning?"

"The Mongolians are all in the open, taking heavy casualties. The private security are using mining equipment as cover. I don't think the Mongolians are going to last much longer."

"And our subjects?"

"They still appear to be in that hole. We don't have an angle on them, and the bird will be out of range in less than sixty seconds."

Dawson cursed. They'd be going in blind. He crested a hill, revealing the mine ahead, a gaping pit of darkness to their right, and a small slice of intense light interspersed with sporadic muzzle bursts to their left. "Got it in sight. Preparing to engage. Zero-One, out."

Acton spotted Arban's head pop up for a split second, the young man having found cover on the opposite side of the earthen ramp, a narrow wedge of ground between the hole and the far wall of the dirt dumped for the access ramp. It was probably the safest place to be. He pointed toward it and Laura nodded.

He waved her ahead and she sprinted past him without hesitation as he pressed against the wall, his AK at the ready, his upper body on a swivel as he watched for anyone who might take a shot. She reached the bottom of the ramp and rushed around it then disappeared for a moment before popping up, a thumb held high. He sighed with relief then raced toward her.

Gunfire suddenly tore into the ground in front of him and he dove, rolling to a knee as he processed the sounds around him, aiming toward where he was certain the gunfire had come from.

And he found Stander in his sights.

He squeezed the trigger, the powerful kick hammering his shoulder as he emptied his mag at the bastard's position. Stander ducked behind the massive wheels, most of Acton's shots ricocheting ineffectually, but they were enough to have Stander taking cover. Acton pushed to his feet, cursing as his mag emptied. He ejected it on the run, then fished a spare from his pocket, glancing toward Stander's position. The man was rising, preparing to take aim, when more shots from ahead erupted.

Acton's head spun toward the new threat and he smiled, Laura the source of fire as she poured lead on Stander's position from a new angle. Stander cried out but Acton didn't look. He leaped over the bottom of the ramp, rolling several times until he dropped behind the opposite side.

THE TOMB OF GENGHIS KHAN

Hands pulled him deeper into the alcove of dirt, and Acton soon realized it was Arban and Elbegdor. Laura dropped back behind the dirt, her job done.

"Thanks!" He gasped and she simply winked at him, extending a hand. Acton grabbed it and gave her three squeezes, their secret I-Love-You message.

She gave him a look. "Ammo?"

He chuckled, giving her his last mag. She reloaded then blew him a kiss. "Love you too!"

Dawson indicated for Niner and Atlas to break left so they could establish a crossfire, then continued forward with Spock and Jack. He spotted a berm that would provide them with good cover and dropped, quickly positioning his MP5 and pressing his eye to the sight, scanning the situation.

He activated his comm. "Let's leave the Mongolians alone. From the right, I've got clear shots on four hostiles, two behind a dump truck, two behind a backhoe, over."

Niner responded. "Copy that. We've got three, all behind an SUV. They're taking the brunt of the Mongolian fire. One appears injured."

"Copy. Make sure whoever you target has a gun in his hand. We don't want to shoot any innocents."

"Roger that."

"Okay, execute in three... two... one... Execute."

Dawson squeezed the trigger, dropping the first target in his arc, then squeezed again, the second going down, as Spock did the same in his. He could hear the report of Niner and Atlas doing the same, then there was silence, broken by a single gunshot, then nothing.

"Okay, let's move in, slowly. Jack, you take the lead. Try to talk down the Mongolians."

Jack gave him a look. "Oh, sure, put the new guy out front."

Spock chuckled. "Trust me, if you were really the new guy, we'd have done a lot worse to you."

Acton slowly rose, the gunfire having stopped far too quickly to make sense. He peered up to see several Mongolian soldiers still in sight, staring about, as confused as he was. One of them spotted him and aimed his weapon at him, shouting something. Acton slowly lowered the weapon to the ground, Laura doing the same, and they all raised their hands as they emerged from their cover, several guns now pointed down at them, everyone above still running on adrenaline and uncertainty.

They were one panicked squeeze of the trigger away from death.

He glanced at Arban. "Ask them what they want us to do."

"Wh-what?"

"In as calm a voice as you can manage, ask them what they want us to do."

"Uh, okay." He said something in Mongolian and the soldier motioned with his weapon, snapping back at Arban. "He wants us to come up."

"Okay, let's everyone do that, nice and slow, hands raised. We're all friends here, there's no need to shoot us." Acton noticed a forced smile on Elbegdor's face. "Don't creep the nice soldiers out with fake smiles. Let's just remain neutral here."

The smile disappeared.

Acton led the way up the ramp, two soldiers standing at the top, their weapons aimed at them, still too jumpy for Acton's liking. Everyone spun at a shout from the darkness. He couldn't understand the words, but he thought he recognized the voice.

And a smile spread at the implications.

Jack had his weapon slung over his back, his hands raised, as he walked toward the bright lights ahead. All guns were trained on him now, and he was about to ask if Major Khurelsukh was among the living when he spotted his body near the chopper.

He cursed.

"Who's in charge?"

A lieutenant stepped forward. "I am. Are you the man our commander betrayed earlier?"

Jack stepped into the light, his hands still raised. "Yes. Call me Jack."

"Then you are involved in this...this desecration?"

Weapons were more forcefully aimed at him and his heart rate ticked up. "Hey, everyone calm down. I'm the one who just saved your asses, okay? You don't think all those guys just shot themselves, do you?"

The lieutenant stared at him, his eyes narrowing. "You did that?"

Jack chuckled, waving a hand at the darkness behind him. "I had friends. May they join me?"

The lieutenant nodded.

"Before they do, can we get everyone to just lower their weapons. We're all friends here. Nobody is going to shoot anybody."

The lieutenant gave the order and the weapons lowered.

Reluctantly.

He smiled regardless. "Excellent." He turned and switched to English. "Okay, you can come out now. Please try to look friendly."

Four shadows emerged, weapons held casually, though he knew from experience these warriors could engage in a split second, eliminating the half-dozen Mongolians that remained with little effort despite their ill-prepared appearance.

Dawson gave them a friendly wave. "Howdy!"

The lieutenant gave him a confused look then repeated the greeting. "Howdy."

Jack smiled, switching back to Mongolian. "See, we're all friends. Now, can you tell me if there's any chance my other friends survived all this?"

The lieutenant shrugged, turning toward the hole dug in the ground. "Bring them up!"

Acton raised his hands a little higher, resuming his climb to the top of the ramp, and as things came into sight, he gasped at the carnage. At least half a dozen soldiers were dead, and he could see bodies on the ground behind some of the nearby equipment. He spotted Jack standing near one of the soldiers who appeared to now be in charge, when his heart leaped into his throat as he spotted four dark figures, armed to the teeth, emerging from the darkness.

"BD!" hissed Laura as she spotted them too.

Acton grabbed her hand. "Don't say anything. We don't know what's going on yet," he whispered, uncertain as to whether they were supposed to play dumb. The situation was still tense, the soldiers clearly still a simple misunderstanding away from laying waste to anything not in a matching uniform.

"Hiya, docs!" called Niner with a wave and a smile.

Acton's shoulders slumped with relief, his question answered. "Hey, Niner. Fancy meeting you here."

The Delta operators continued to approach, smiles on their faces, completely relaxed.

And it was having an effect.

Acton decided the best way to settle things down was to mix the civilians with the new arrivals, and took Laura's hand, stepping toward their old friends.

"We were vacationing at a nearby spa," said Spock. "Thought we'd drop in and say hi."

Acton laughed, as did Laura, her lilt relaxing everyone. She gave Niner a hug and he lifted her off the ground as he usually did, eliciting a giggle. Handshakes and hugs were exchanged, and Acton noted they all remained in positions that would provide them with complete coverage should something go south.

He waved at Jack. "Glad you came back."

"Was there ever any doubt?"

"Tremendous."

Jack laughed. "I never leave a man behind. At least not for long."

More words were exchanged in Mongolian, and Acton beckoned Arban to join them. Arban walked over and Acton put a protective arm around him, noting all the Mongolian weapons were now aimed at the ground or slung over their shoulders.

Acton turned to Jack. "We need to have a conversation." He gestured at the man Jack had been speaking with. "Is he in charge?"

"Yes, this is Lieutenant Jalair."

"Okay, we have a problem here."

Dawson's eyes narrowed. "What?"

"In that hole over there is the tomb of Genghis Khan."

Spock cocked an eyebrow. "*The* Genghis Khan?"

"The one and only."

Dawson frowned. "Are you sure?"

"Pretty."

"Shit. I'm guessing that's important."

"It's what this has all been about. The agreement with the Mongolian government is that if the mine finds anything of archaeological importance, they're to cease operations until it can be assessed. It could even result in the entire operation being shut down."

Niner whistled. "From what I've read, this is a pretty big operation."

"Massive," agreed Arban. "And expanding several fold." He jerked a thumb over his shoulder at Elbegdor, still standing at the top of the ramp. "That's why they bribed him to look the other way, but even he changed his mind once he realized what we had found."

Dawson stated the obvious. "Do we care?"

Acton's eyebrows shot up. "What kind of question is that? Of course we care!"

Dawson shook his head. "No, Doc, I mean, do *we*, as in covert operatives of the American government, on foreign soil without the permission or knowledge of the Mongolian government, care? Can we extract you two now, and leave this for the Mongolians to sort out?"

Acton closed his eyes for a moment as Laura squeezed his hand. They were both thinking the same thing. He desperately wanted to stay, to try and save that which Stander had almost destroyed, but Dawson was right. This wasn't their business. It was up to the Mongolians to sort things out. His lone reason to remain was curiosity, and that had killed too many cats over the years.

He sighed. "You're right. We're not needed here."

"Good." Dawson turned to Spock. "Go retrieve the chopper."

Spock gave a two-fingered salute and disappeared into the darkness, Jack explaining what was going on to the lieutenant who appeared pleased that the foreigners would soon be gone. Orders were barked and the surviving Mongolians began loading their dead into the Hind, when Niner cleared his throat.

"Umm, BD, we've got company."

He nodded toward the massive pit and everyone turned, Laura gasping at the sight of hundreds of men emerging from the darkness.

"Who the hell are they?" asked Jack.

"They're the mineworkers," said Arban. "Their barracks are on the far side of the pit. They must have heard what was going on."

Acton shook his head. "And they walked *toward* the gunfire?"

Arban's eyes widened and he rushed toward the lieutenant, rapidly delivering his urgent message, whatever that was, and the lieutenant's eyes bulged. He barked orders at his men who rushed toward the new arrivals, firing rounds over their heads, sending them scattering back into the night.

Acton turned to Arban, horrified. "What was that all about?"

"They can't see what we found. Nobody can."

"Why? They have a right to know!"

Arban shook his head. "You don't understand." He left the group and joined the still solitary Elbegdor, an intense conversation taking place between the two.

Jack stepped over. "What the hell is going on now?"

Acton shook his head. "I wish I knew."

"What will happen here? The truth."

"The truth?" Elbegdor sighed. "The truth is that no matter what we want, this mine will continue to operate. No matter what was found here today, there is simply too much money involved, too many people who have been bribed."

"What will they do with the Khan's body?"

"I fear they'll destroy it. At a minimum, they'll take it to the capital and put it on display."

"Despite those who would oppose it?"

Elbegdor shrugged. "I really can't say. Perhaps they'll try to keep it a secret, but you know how secrets are. The bigger they are, the more likely they'll come out."

Arban's shoulders slumped. "Then there's only one thing we can do." He looked up as a helicopter approached, its lights intentionally on so as not to surprise anyone. It landed at the edge of the lit area and the pilot, one of the American soldiers, climbed out, leaving it powered up for their impending departure.

Something pressed against his back.

"Don't move."

"Oh no!"

It was Laura who saw it first. Everyone turned and Acton instinctively placed himself between her and Stander, now at the top of the ramp, a knife pressed against Conrad's throat, a pistol against Arban's back, his upper arm oozing blood from Laura's earlier shot.

"Now, everybody just remain calm. I'm going to get on that chopper with my friends here, then you can all go about your business."

All weapons were now trained on the mercenary, but he didn't appear concerned as he hustled his captives toward the means of escape Spock had just brought him.

"I've got a shot. Do I take it?" whispered Niner.

Acton whispered his own response. "You could hit the kid. He's innocent in all this."

Niner ignored him. "BD. What do you want me to do?"

"Hold your fire. The moment that gun is off the kid, take the shot."

"Roger that." Niner slowly fell back into the darkness, Atlas following, as Stander took his prisoners behind the massive Hind gunship, the soldiers following him.

Dawson repositioned, anticipating Stander's next move. "Jack, tell the lieutenant to have his men hold their position."

Jack repeated the request without hesitation, the lieutenant hissing the order to his men. They stopped, and Stander emerged out the other side, now only feet from the idling chopper. He suddenly removed the weapon from Arban's back and fired several shots at a nearby generator, the diesel engine sparking then sputtering to a halt, the entire area swamped in darkness, the only lights now the blinding ones from the chopper.

"I've got no shot!" called Niner as the chopper powered up.

"Hold your fire!" ordered Dawson as it lifted off. Dawson and Spock rushed forward as the chopper banked away, heading rapidly into the darkness. Acton ran over to join them as flashlights played out over the ground.

Revealing nobody.

Acton's shoulders slumped. "He has them."

The Hind powered up as the soldiers rapidly finished the grim task of loading their dead comrades, the lieutenant jogging over, saying something to Jack.

Jack jerked a thumb over his shoulder at the gunship. "This is our last ride out of here for a while. Shall we?"

Dawson nodded. "Everybody on board." Acton was about to protest when Dawson shook his head. "No exceptions."

Acton frowned, but agreed, the Delta operators, along with Jack, their rescued hostages, and Elbegdor, all boarding, leaving the mine abandoned to its workers.

He just prayed they left the tomb alone until someone in authority could return.

And that Arban would be okay.

En route to Ulaanbaatar, Mongolia

Acton gripped his seat as the Hind blasted through the air, the unbelievable din apparently suffered only by him and Laura. "Is he actually trying to catch him?" he asked Niner, sitting beside him.

"I hope so, otherwise my fillings are being shaken loose for no good reason."

"How can something this big catch the other chopper?"

"This is military. It'll top out at about a hundred-eighty knots. That civilian job is old. Maybe one-fifty. We'll be caught up in no time."

"Then what?"

Niner shrugged. "That's up to the Mongolians. Blow them out of the sky, track them, encourage them to land."

Acton's eyes narrowed. "Encourage them?"

"Fire a shot across the bow, so to speak."

"Do you think that would work with someone like Stander?"

"Never met the man. It'd work with me."

"You're not crazy."

Niner extended a hand. "Hi, my name's Niner. Nice to meet you."

Acton laughed, batting the hand away. The pilot shouted something and Dawson rose, joining Jack and the lieutenant near the cockpit.

"Must have spotted them."

Acton tensed. "Now what?"

"Now we see what choice they make."

Dawson pursed his lips. If it were only Stander ahead of them, he'd blow him out of the sky, but there were civilians, though from what he had been told, only one was innocent in all this. Conrad would be going to prison for a long time, and Dawson hoped it was a Mongolian one rather than a cushy American one. Stander should just be executed, but he'd likely be tossed in the same prison, or extradited somewhere that had wanted him for a long time.

The lieutenant shouted something and the weapons system officer opened fire, tracers mixed with bullets streaking across the night sky, directly ahead of the chopper. It banked to the right then resumed its course.

"Where's he heading?"

"Ulaanbaatar."

Dawson nodded. "He thinks he can land then lose himself in the city."

Jack shrugged. "One-point-five million souls. Definitely possible."

"How far are we?"

"Not even halfway. Plenty of time to stop him."

Dawson grunted. "If we're not willing to shoot, then he'll make it."

Jack regarded him for a moment. "What do you want to do?"

Dawson shook his head. "Not my call."

"But if it were?"

"Let him get to where he's going. We've got almost a dozen men here. He lands, we land, you call in for reinforcements, they block off the area and we take him down."

"That's what I'd do too."

Dawson nodded at the lieutenant. "Then you better convince him."

Approaching Ulaanbaatar, Mongolia

It felt like the longest flight of Acton's life, but finally the lights of the city could be seen in the distance. He gripped Laura's hand as Bravo Team readied themselves, the lieutenant having apparently agreed to let them take the lead. Military and police units across the city had been notified, but nobody knew where Stander intended to land. It had to be somewhere densely populated, where he could lose himself among the crowd, though as Acton checked his watch, he realized there likely was no place for him to do so.

Everyone was asleep.

Dawson turned to his team. "Okay, the kid is the only subject we're concerned about. If Conrad is the meat shield and things go south, then take the shot. If you get Stander, great, if you miss, take a second shot. Conrad should be on the ground. If it's the kid, we try to contain. Copy?"

"Yes, Sergeant Major!"

Something was shouted and Jack translated. "He's landing!"

"Where?"

"Airfield. He must think he can steal a plane!"

Niner's eyes widened. "Is he nuts?"

Doors slid open and Dawson took his position. "Okay, everybody set!"

The chopper bounced and Bravo Team leaped out of sight.

Dawson rushed forward with Spock to his right, Niner and Atlas covering the left as the door of the stolen helicopter was thrown open and Stander appeared, pulling Conrad with him. Dawson peered into the cockpit but couldn't find Arban.

Yet it didn't matter.

Conrad was the shield.

Stander held Conrad tight, revealing little of his body as he kept his head hidden behind his hostage's, the gun pressed against the base of his skull, not even leaving a shoulder to target.

Yet.

"Everybody back off, or he dies."

Conrad was in a panic, his eyes bulging with fear. "Do what he says! Please! I'll pay you anything! I'll make you all very rich men!"

Stander sneered. "Yes, listen to him. We'll all be rich. Just let me get out of here." He shoved his weapon a little harder against Conrad. "Now, just everybody back off!"

Dawson kept advancing, his weapon raised, still no shot, but Niner and Atlas were flanking their target, and if they succeeded, this would all be over in moments.

Stander turned slightly. "Tell those two to hold their position or he's dead."

Dawson whispered into his comm. "Hold position." He kept advancing, heading slightly to the right, forcing Stander to turn, his back now to Niner's position. "Just let him go, and everyone lives."

"I have no intention of spending the rest of my days in a Mongolian prison."

"I don't see many options in your future that you're going to like."

"Got the shot," whispered Niner in his comm.

And Stander knew.

He fired, Conrad collapsing in a heap, blood rushing from the cavity now in his head, as Stander dropped his weapon, raising his hands in the air, a smile on his face. "I—"

"Taking the shot." Dawson squeezed the trigger.

"Clear!"

Acton leaped from the chopper as soon as Jack ushered them out, helping Laura before running toward the carnage. Stander and Conrad were dead, just behind the chopper, and he could honestly say he couldn't care less. "Where's Arban?"

Atlas emerged from poking his head in the chopper. "He's not here."

"What? Where the hell is he?"

Laura gasped. "You don't think…"

Acton looked at her. "What?"

"Well, we know he was on board. If he's not now, then…"

And Acton knew exactly what she was thinking. He spun toward Dawson. "We have to go back."

Dawson eyed him. "Why?"

"Stander must have thrown him out of the chopper. He could be lying on the ground out there, injured."

Dawson shook his head. "Doc, we were traveling at over a hundred-fifty miles per hour at several hundred feet. If he was tossed, I hate to say it, he's dead."

Acton cursed, slamming his fist into the chopper's windshield, for Dawson was right. Tears flowed down Laura's cheeks and he took her in his arms, holding tight as his own ran. Their entire purpose had been to save the young man they barely knew, and they had failed, his final moments probably the most terrifying he could imagine.

He sniffed, then drew a deep breath. "We have to tell his wife."

Dawson shook his head. "No, we're getting you out of here. Now. We've got a plane waiting." He stared past Acton and cursed.

Acton turned to see what had Dawson concerned, and tensed as two military transports rolled up, two dozen men jumping out of the rear, quickly surrounding the area. An officer rushed forward, barking orders as Dawson indicated for his men to keep their weapons lowered. The man stepped over to Dawson after the lieutenant pointed him out.

"You are American soldiers?"

"We're not Mongolian."

Not a lie, technically.

The new arrival pointed at their private charter. "You arrived on that?"

"Yes."

"Then you leave. Now. Mongolian government thank you for your assistance."

Dawson bowed his head. "You're welcome." He indicated for his men to head for the plane, then beckoned Acton and Laura to follow.

"No. They stay here. You four leave."

Dawson squared his shoulders. "I'm not leaving without them."

An order was barked, two dozen guns raised. "You leave. Now." The man stepped closer. "Or you don't."

Dawson appeared calm, holding up his hand then tapping his pocket. "May I?"

The man nodded.

Dawson pulled out his phone, finding a piece of pertinent intel, then turned to Acton. "According to my records, your travel agent has you booked on a flight six hours from now. Try to be on it. We'll work the problem as soon as we're in the air."

"Okay." Acton held Laura tight as Dawson and the others were forced to leave at gunpoint, their equipment confiscated. Jack strolled over. "Now what?"

Jack shrugged. "Dunno. Didn't plan on this."

"Nothing seems to be going to plan." Acton frowned then stared at the helicopter, picturing a terrified Arban falling to his death.

You poor kid.

Mine Site, Eastern Mongolia

One hour earlier

Arban crouched in the tall grass, watching as the helicopter left, leaving him all alone to do what needed to be done. The moment the lights had gone dim, he had elbowed Stander in the stomach and lost himself in the night, taking cover, hoping against hope everyone would think he had been taken with Conrad.

And it had worked.

The spirits were truly on his side.

And he had no time to waste.

With the military gone, the workers could return at any moment. He rushed down the ramp, stumbling in the darkness, his eyes still adjusting to the moonlight, then climbed behind the still idling loader, its precious cargo still in its scoop.

Elbegdor was right. The mine would go on, there would be no preserving this site, which meant the great shaman's remains must be moved, moved to a location that no one would know about, as the great leader had wanted.

He climbed in the loader, its cabin lit, and stared at the controls, soon figuring out how to at least get the vehicle to move. The bucket he would worry about later. He approached the ramp, realizing later was now, and struggled for a few minutes before raising the bucket. He climbed the ramp, his heart hammering at how close he was to the edges, then breathed a heavy sigh of relief as he crested the top, the entire machine bouncing horribly as he flattened out. He hammered on the gas, heading to what he hoped was the east, and slowly increased his speed, his final destination not yet known, but when it was, it would be to him only.

The great Genghis Khan, shaman to his people, would rest in peace once more, with only one soul left to know where his remains were buried.

Incheon International Airport

Incheon, South Korea

Reading rubbed his eyes as he shuffled off the airplane. The eleven-hour flight had been horrible, despite sitting in business class. The seat was fine, it was the nightmares and worry that had been the problem. He was consumed with concern over his friends.

In these moments of self-pity, he focused on how little he had in life. He felt old and used up. He was divorced, though he had a great son finally allowing him to participate in his life, and he had a couple of great friends who lived on the wrong side of the pond.

Other than that, what did he have?

He hated his job, though kept doing it to have something to occupy his time. Yes, Michelle was a great partner, but she was decades his junior, and they were work friends only.

She's no Martin.

Detective Inspector Martin Chaney had been his junior partner when Reading was a Detective Chief Inspector at Scotland Yard. It had taken time, but eventually they had become friends in and out of the office, grabbing pints together or sharing takeaway while watching a senselessly violent movie together.

Their favorite was Lethal Weapon 2.

And he *was* getting too old for this shit.

Yet he was doing it to save the last two real friends he had in the world. Acton and Laura were in his thoughts constantly, the things they had been through, good and bad, creating bonds that would never be broken. He had been there for their first kiss and their marriage. They had included him in everything, never asking for anything in return.

They were incredible people.

People he had tried to arrest when they all first met.

He smiled at the memory.

Please, God, let them be okay.

His phone vibrated in his pocket and he grabbed it as he strode down the jetway. He swiped his thumb. "Hello?"

"Agent Reading, this is Chris. Good flight?"

"I'm getting too old for this shit."

Leroux laughed. "I did recommend you stay in London."

"And I said bollocks to that. Any word?"

"Unfortunately, things have gone south."

Reading's stomach flipped. "What happened?"

"The professors are in local custody and our team has been sent back to South Korea at gunpoint. We're trying to find out what's going on, but not having much luck. Just hold tight and we'll keep you posted."

"Okay, let me know."

He ended the call and dialed Michelle.

"Hello?"

"Do it."

"Consider it done."

Genghis Khan International Airport

Ulaanbaatar, Mongolia

"I can't stop thinking about Arban."

Acton tore his eyes away from the door of the small room they had been sitting in for hours with no contact from anyone, local or otherwise. He took Laura's hand and squeezed it. "Me neither. What a horrible way to die. At least it would have been quick."

"Would it? I mean, I suppose it could be depending upon how he hit the ground, but is there a chance he could have survived, even for just a few minutes?"

Jack stuffed another piece of gum in his mouth, the man obviously suffering from some sort of addiction or affectation. "Nah, there's no way. You're thinking of falls down the side of a mountain or something. They only survive those because they hit things on the way down."

"What about parachutists where their chute doesn't open?"

Jack shook his head. "You're forgetting they usually have a shitty chute trailing behind them killing some of their velocity, but they also didn't start from a speed of about one-fifty. Your friend would have been pushed out at full speed, maintained most of that forward momentum, while gaining vertical speed as he dropped. I'm sorry to say—or rather happy, I guess—that he would have hit hard and died likely on impact. If he survived, it would have been only to bleed out from many wounds, and he wouldn't have known what was going on—or felt anything—after a few seconds." He frowned. "I suppose there's some comfort in that."

Acton sighed. "I keep thinking about what that Elbegdor guy said, that because we showed up, Arban had to die."

Laura frowned. "Me too."

Jack shook his head, an exasperated sigh escaping. "What is it with you two? The glass is always half empty!" He leaned forward. "Listen, the guy was in trouble and he reached out. Obviously to the right people, because you managed to get people like me involved. Things didn't work out. Sometimes the plan doesn't always come together. Right now, we need to focus on how we're getting you two safely out of here."

Acton regarded him. "What about you?"

Jack shrugged. "I never worry about myself. If I get out, I get out. If not, oh well, life's a bitch. My only job here is to get the two of you out. That might mean walking you onto an airplane, or giving you the opportunity to walk yourselves onto one. Either way, live or die, my job is done."

Acton grunted. "Any idea how you're going to do that?"

Jack popped another piece of gum in his mouth. "Workin' on it."

"It still doesn't change the fact Arban is dead," said Laura. "And his poor wife has no idea." She closed her eyes. "That poor woman." She opened them and turned to Acton. "The first chance we get we call her and let her know."

"Absolutely." He checked his watch. "You know, that flight we're booked on leaves in less than an hour."

Laura frowned. "Doesn't look like we're going to be on it."

Jack popped yet another piece of gum. "Never lose hope, my friends. Things are always afoot."

Laura regarded him. "You seem confident."

Jack shrugged. "You survive this long in the business, you figure someone must be watching over you."

"God?"

Jack chuckled. "Control."

Acton drew a breath, his heart rate ticking up at the idea, then checked his watch again. "Well, let's just hope your Control knows we're here and has some clout."

"Don't worry about it. You're innocent professors. The State Department will eventually get you out. The worst you have to worry about is being tossed in a prison cell for a while. Me, I'm a spy, but don't tell anyone. They're liable to shoot me if things go wrong."

Laura smiled. "Yet you're still confident."

Another shrug. "Beats being worried all the time. Look at you two. You're both miserable, you're fidgeting, you're clearly worrying yourselves to death. Then look at me. Cool, calm, and collected. The picture of serenity."

The door opened and they flinched.

Including Jack.

Two armed guards entered, and something was yelled at Jack.

He smiled at Acton and Laura. "Well, I guess it's off to the firing squad for me." He rose then bowed at them, popping another piece of chewing gum into his mouth, the pack the only thing the guards had agreed to let him keep. "A pleasure meeting the both of you. I hope things work out better for you."

He left, but as he did, Acton noticed him put his fingers to his mouth, then press his hand against the door frame. The door shut, leaving them alone.

Laura looked at him. "What do we do now?"

Acton glanced about the room for the umpteenth time, still not spotting any cameras. "Remember what he said about creating an opportunity for us to get ourselves on that flight?"

"Yes?"

He rose, stepped over to the door, then tried the handle. The door opened. He pulled it a couple of inches, spotting the wad of gum stuck in the mortise, and smiled. He glanced back at Laura. "I say we try to get out of here."

"We'll never get on our flight. We don't have our passports, ID, nothing."

He shook his head. "Forget the flight. If we can reach the embassy, then we should be fine."

Laura rose. "Or dead."

"I've always thought it would be romantic if we died together."

She grunted. "My idea of romantic is in bed, ninety years old, holding hands."

He shrugged. "To each their own."

He pulled open the door and stepped out with purpose, praying to God this wasn't the stupidest thing they had ever done.

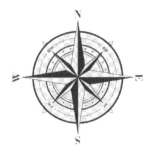

Incheon International Airport

Incheon, South Korea

None of them were happy. In fact, they were all pissed off and disappointed in themselves. The entire flight back had been spent playing the blame game, then second-guessing what they could have done. By the time they landed, they had figured out how they could have taken down all two dozen opponents with a minimal chance of friendly casualties.

And it was BS.

A million things would have had to go right, and just one thing wrong.

They had been given no choice. If the entire team had been there, no problem. But with only four men, the odds were impossible, and against their ROEs.

The Mongolians weren't going to shoot first, because they knew they had the superior numbers.

The only way they could have come out on top would be for all four of them to open fire, full-auto, each covering an arc perfectly, no overlap.

Creating an international incident, violating orders, and likely failing regardless.

No, there was nothing they could do.

Officially.

As soon as they were in a secure room, he turned to one of their escorts. "Phone."

The man handed one over and Dawson dialed Control, their comm gear confiscated before they were allowed onto their charter, and using a civilian frequency from the cockpit out of the question.

Leroux responded immediately. "Control here."

"This is Bravo Zero-One. Tell me you've got something, or I'm going on vacation and getting them myself."

"All we know at the moment is that the Mongolians are acknowledging they have them in their custody."

"No shit. There were eyewitnesses."

"True, but this is good news. The fact they're not denying it means they're probably just going to make a stink that your team was there, demand an apology, then hand them over. I don't think they're at real risk, unless…"

Dawson's eyes narrowed. "Unless?"

"You know those two. They're definitely going to try something stupid if they're given the chance."

Dawson grunted in agreement. If he knew the professors, they were already up to something. "If I were you, I'd be letting the US and British embassies know they should be expecting them without passports."

Leroux chuckled. "Already done. They're waiting for them, and they've both sent reps to the airport just in case they're still there."

"And what about Jack?"

"Him, they're not acknowledging. They know who and what he is, so that's expected."

Dawson frowned, not liking what he was hearing. "Are we just abandoning him?"

"No, but right now we're not making any waves until the professors are secure."

"And that mining operation? What about the kid that disappeared? Any sign of him?"

"Negative. We scanned the route and didn't pick up any heat signatures. There's no point now that it's daytime, the body will be cold by now. We did find something interesting, though."

Hope was piqued. "What's that?"

"The loader you said was used to scoop up the tomb?"

"Yeah?"

"It's missing."

His eyes widened. "What?"

"It's gone."

Dawson shook his head, holding up a hand to cut off the questions the others were about to ask. "What about the contents of the bucket?"

"No idea. We can't tell if it was dumped or taken with it, but the loader is gone."

Dawson thought back on the situation. "There were a lot of miners there that were curious. Do you think they could have stolen it after everyone left?"

"Possible, though what would they do with it? It's a million dollar piece of equipment and there's not much of a market for it in the area. It would probably get traced back to its original owners fairly quickly."

Dawson smiled as a thought occurred to him, a thought he had a feeling the far cleverer Leroux already had. "You think the kid took it."

"It's a possibility. You said you never actually saw him get in the helicopter with Stander."

"None of us did."

"So, if he managed to escape at the mine and hide, he might still be alive. And with his feelings about the situation, perhaps he decided to take the body and bury it somewhere else."

"Should we try to find it?"

"No, I think we just leave it be. It's an internal Mongolian matter. If they want to find it, they can. As far as we're concerned, this operation is limited to getting the professors and Jack out of the country."

Dawson regarded the others. "Well, let the powers that be know we're all willing to go back right now if they'll let us." Three heads bobbed in vigorous agreement.

"They already know. And Sergeant Major?"

"Yes?"

"Please stay put. I've already got one rogue Interpol Agent who's off doing God knows what. I don't want to have to worry about you guys too."

Dawson grunted. "I make no promises."

Genghis Khan International Airport

Ulaanbaatar, Mongolia

Kane pushed the broom, sweeping the dust and detritus of the windswept parking lot, his head down, his shoulders rounded, a six-foot Caucasian sticking out like a sore thumb in Mongolia, especially when disguised as a manual laborer.

He had flown in commercial from Beijing minutes before, and all indications from Langley were that Acton and Laura were still in custody at the airport, diplomatic games underway.

But no one had any idea where, and running about secure areas trying doors was one surefire way to get oneself shot in the process.

Though there was one person who might know, and according to the observers on the ground from the embassy, he should still be inside the building.

Jack.

The airport was small by international standards, with few ways in and out, all being watched, all having had nothing resembling police or military leave since shortly after Delta had been forced out of the country.

That could have gone south in a hurry.

He had been a member of Bravo Team years ago, recruited out of the Unit by the CIA, and had few regrets about his decision until he met Fang. She was the first woman he had loved, and the first woman who knew what he really did for a living—and understood the sacrifices, as she had been Special Forces herself.

Just for the wrong team.

But now that he was in a serious, committed relationship, he sometimes wished he were back in Delta, mostly stateside, deployed with a group of buddies who always had your back.

Instead of out here, alone.

Or worse, like Jack, wondering if someone had been sent in to save your ass, or if you had been disavowed to avoid the embarrassment of an international incident.

Fortunately for Jack, he was his secondary mission objective, though to achieve his primary, he needed intel that he was certain Jack had.

A secure door opened nearby and four soldiers emerged, two holding Jack between them, heading directly for a group of military vehicles to his left. He shoved the pile of dirt ahead of him, turning into their path, one of the soldiers shouting at him, probably to get out of the way.

Kane rose to his full height as his foot pressed down on the end of the broom. He twisted the broomstick loose as his smile spread. Jack's eyes widened slightly. "Howdy boys."

He snapped the stick forward with his right hand, catching the nearest guard on the chin, and as he did, he advanced, swinging the other end forward, impacting the side of the head on one of those holding Jack.

Giving the trained operative an opportunity.

Kane ignored the other soldier holding Jack—he was now Jack's responsibility. Kane whipped the stick high then down, cracking it over the fourth guard then snap-kicked the first in the neck, sending him to the ground coughing. He grabbed the fourth in a sleeper hold and had him out in short order as Jack engaged his man, the other two still down and out for the moment.

Kane dropped his target, unconscious, then stepped forward and placed a shoe on the carotid artery of the second man, rendering him unconscious as Jack finally took his man down.

"Took you long enough." Kane booted the first man in the head, knocking him out cold.

Jack held up his zip-tied hands. "I did have a handicap."

"Excuses, excuses." Kane drew a small knife and cut the bindings. "Let's get these guys out of sight."

They dragged them between the parked vehicles, rolling them under, then Kane surveyed the area.

"What's the plan?"

"First things first. Where are the professors?"

Jack gave him a look. "How did I know all this effort wasn't on my behalf?"

"You know Langley. They only come for one of us if they need something." He pointed toward a service entrance and they jogged toward it.

"That's why I always try to have something they need."

Kane laughed. "Yup, always hold something back, and make sure they know." They reached the door and Kane picked the lock. "So, where are they?"

"Last I saw them, they were in Room 108. Through that door they took me out of over there, go straight then take your first right then second left. That should put you in the right corridor."

Kane pulled the door open. "Okay, first right, second left. Room 108. Got it." They stepped inside and headed deeper into the complex until Kane found what he was looking for.

The baggage sorting area.

He checked the tags on one of the already loaded baggage carriers, then pointed. "In you go. Get yourself on the plane. The cargo hold will be pressurized, but you might get a little chilly." He patted one of the bags. "I'm sure you can find something comfy to snuggle up in."

Jack shook his head. "Some plan!"

"Hey, if you wanted upgraded seats, you should have asked beforehand."

Jack shook his hand. "Thanks for this, whoever the hell you are."

Kane grinned. "Just get your ass out of here, and maybe someday I'll tell you who you owe half your pension check to."

Jack climbed on top of the carrier. "Pension check? You actually plan on living that long?"

Kane shrugged. "When you have the right reason."

Jack regarded him for a moment. "You're a lucky man." He dropped down, pulling a couple of bags overtop him. "Now get your ass out of here and save those professors. I don't want their lives on my conscience."

"Good luck!"

Kane made a beeline across the building, eventually reaching the corridor that led to the door he had seen Jack escorted out of. He soon found room 108 and tried the door.

It opened.

A little too easily.

He checked inside, finding it empty, then noticed the gum on the door, blocking the bolt.

That's got Jack written all over it.

He cursed as he shook his head, heading quickly back toward the public area of the terminal. There was little doubt the professors were attempting their own escape. If the guards had tried the door, they would have discovered it wasn't closed properly, and then found the gum. It would have been removed, along with the professors.

But the fact the gum remained, suggested they had escaped, and the fact nobody seemed excited by that, meant no one knew.

Where the hell would they go?

Langley had told him they were booked on a flight that would be leaving in under an hour, though there was no way they'd be able to board. They wouldn't have their passports, and they'd be caught if they attempted to board without them.

And they'd know that.

If they had stayed put, he could have given them the passports he had on him, and slipped them on board using the two tickets Langley had purchased under their new identities. Before the Mongolians could have figured out what was going on, they'd be halfway to Seoul.

But all that was moot now.

Where are you two heading?

There was only one possibility he could think of.

Well, two.

The US or British Embassies.

It's where he would go, and he had learned long ago that those two thought like spies.

Too many movies.

He merged into the public, the terminal fairly busy now that the sun had been up for hours and flights were moving in and out. He scanned the crowd, but saw nothing.

Suddenly someone shouted something, then another. Screams broke out to his right and the crowds sprinted toward him, panic on their faces. He headed toward the excitement, dodging in and out of the crowd, remaining at the periphery and not obvious to any who might be watching.

Then cursed as he saw the source of all the excitement.

James Acton and Laura Palmer, standing near the exit, their hands held high, surrounded by nearly a dozen armed men.

If only you had waited.

Laura raised her hands, trying to remain calm and not panic. This wasn't the first time guns had been pointed at her, and it wouldn't be the last. Though these security personnel did not seem happy, and too many were practicing poor trigger discipline.

Too many fingers were on the triggers.

One false move, one nervous tick, and they were dead.

"Perhaps trying to escape wasn't such a wise move."

James stood with his back pressed against hers, his hands high. "Now you tell me?"

She suppressed a chuckle, not wanting to piss anyone off with the notion she wasn't taking their predicament seriously. "I didn't mention it before?"

"Who can remember these things." James turned so he could see her. "There is one good thing, though."

Her eyes narrowed. "There is?"

He nodded past the soldiers. "Look."

She turned to see what he was talking about and smiled. Scores of people were gathered, hugging walls, cowering behind pillars, and hiding behind the screens of their cellphones as they recorded their fifteen minutes of fame.

"They can't shoot us. Not now."

Laura wasn't so certain. "Well, they can, but at least we'll make the news."

"Out of my way!" shouted somebody through the crowd to their left. "I said, out of my way!"

They both turned to see the source of the commotion, but she already knew. She would recognize that voice anywhere. Her face brightened at the sight of the burly Reading shoving through the crowd as he waved a sheaf of papers over his head.

"We don't know him," hissed James, and she wiped the elation off her face.

"Who's in charge here?" demanded the Interpol Agent and their good friend. An officer stepped forward, snapping his heels together, the man nearly a full foot shorter than Reading, who inflated his barrel-chested frame the moment he saw the man.

Reading was double his size.

Easily.

"Do you speak English?"

The man nodded, though still hadn't spoken a word of it.

"Bloody wonderful." He showed him his Interpol ID. "I'm Agent Reading of Interpol." He shook the pages. "I have international arrest warrants for these malcontents."

A grin almost slipped.

Malcontents?

Reading stabbed a finger in their direction. "James Acton and Laura Palmer are wanted for international wire fraud, money laundering, and a whole host of other criminal acts in the United States and the United Kingdom. Per international treaty and convention, I hereby request you hand them both over to my custody, so that I can return them to their respective homelands for immediate prosecution."

The officer stared at the paperwork, leaving Laura to wonder if he could read or even speak English.

It didn't matter.

The paperwork was shoved back in Reading's hands and orders barked. Four men advanced then holstered their weapons. They cuffed her and James, then pushed them toward Reading.

Reading took them each by an arm and bowed his head at the officer. "Thank you for your cooperation." He led them toward the gate their regularly scheduled flight was to depart from in less than half an hour, and were allowed on board after a hasty discussion between the officer and the poor women manning the gate. Three seats together were made available, and Reading none too gently pushed James into the window seat, helped Laura into the middle, then sat in the aisle seat. He leaned over as if to check James' lap belt then gave them both a look.

"Keep your bloody mouths shut until we land."

Incheon International Airport

Incheon, South Korea

The flight had seemed interminably long, but Acton had kept his mouth shut the entire time. He figured if it was okay to talk, Reading would. And their friend didn't.

How he had become involved, he was dying to know. They hadn't seen hide nor hair of Kane, though obviously his message had got through, since the Delta team had arrived just in time to save the day.

Or most of the day.

Arban was dead, and they had nearly become prisoners in a country not known for a model penal system.

All in all, it had been a bad two days.

Dawson had told them during the long chopper ride from the mine that Tommy and Mai were safely out of the country, the one thing that had gone right, though apparently there were issues there as well.

Too many were dead, including innocents. Lives had been destroyed, and he would live with the knowledge that their meddling had cost a young man his life.

We should have just stayed home and let Dylan deal with it.

If they had waited, then perhaps Kane's contacts could have done something to save Arban, yet even if they couldn't, all indications were that Arban might have been allowed to live.

Yet that wasn't true. If he and Laura hadn't gone to Mongolia, then Jack would have never paid a corrupt Mongolian officer to use his helicopter to catch up to them, would never have been double-crossed, and never have taken them to the mine, putting a dozen Mongolian soldiers on the scene.

And if those soldiers hadn't been there, and Bravo Team hadn't arrived, the private security would have been the only ones with the guns.

Once Elbegdor realized what the find was, he had changed his mind on how things should proceed, and Stander and Conrad would surely have killed him along with Arban, then destroyed one of the greatest archaeological finds in history.

He closed his eyes and sighed.

No matter what, Arban would have died, and it wasn't their fault.

Yet guilt still consumed him, guilt he hoped would fade with the perspective time brought.

The door to the Korean Air flight finally opened and the flight crew had everyone remain in their seats as Reading led them off the plane and down the jetway. They were met by South Korean police and escorted to a secure section of the building and put into a room. Reading remained outside for a couple of moments, then entered and closed the door.

He tossed the handcuff keys on the table. "I should have left you two there."

Laura unlocked her cuffs then did the same for Acton. "You would have never forgiven yourself." She rose and gave the big man a hug and a kiss on the cheek. Acton rose and gave the man a thumping hug and leaned in for a kiss. Reading recoiled.

"Don't you bloody dare."

Acton laughed, winking at Laura, then everyone sat. Acton regarded his friend. "Care to explain what the hell just happened? How did you pull that off?"

"Well, I'll probably lose my job for this, but I had Michelle create fake arrest warrants."

Acton spun a finger backward. "Whoa whoa, just back up the truck a second. How did you find out?"

"Rita."

Acton's eyes narrowed. "Rita? Rita Perdok?"

Reading nodded. "She called me yesterday, told me that Tommy and Mai were trying to get some GPS coordinates to Dylan, and they didn't know how. Rita reached out to me, I passed them on to Dylan through the app, and then booked a flight here. When I arrived, Leroux told me you had been arrested. Before I left, I had Michelle prep the fake warrants. I called her, had her put them in the system, I printed them off at an Internet café here, then got on the first flight to Mongolia. I waited for some disturbance that I was sure you would make if things went wrong, and you know the rest."

Laura's head slowly bobbed then stopped. "Wait, why would Rita be calling you? Wouldn't she call Greg?"

Reading shifted in his chair. "I'm afraid I've got some bad news—"

Acton's stomach flipped and his chest heaved. "Please don't—!"

Reading rapidly waved his hands in front of him. "No! No! He's not dead! But he was badly beaten and tortured."

Acton's shoulders slumped and Laura leaned against him, her head on his shoulder, tears breaking out.

"What happened?"

"I'm not entirely sure, but from what I've been able to gather, he came to check on your house and someone was there waiting for you. He beat him quite badly, and…"

Acton's eyes were burning as he struggled to maintain control, mental images of his best friend's brutalization overwhelming him. "And?"

"There's a chance he might not walk again."

He lost it, collapsing onto the table as his entire body was racked with sobs. Laura fell on top of him, crying, and Reading reached out, gently holding his arm and hers.

"It's my fault," cried Acton. "I should have stayed put. I never should have gone to Mongolia."

"It's our fault," said Laura. "If anyone's to blame, it's both of us."

Reading patted their arms. "Bollocks. It's the man who did it. And you'll be happy to know Sherrie and Fang caught him. He'll pay for his crimes."

Acton sniffed, rising then wiping his tears from his face. He put an arm around Laura and held her tight as he regained his composure. "I have to call him."

Reading reached for his phone when the door opened, Tommy and Mai entering, both rushing into their arms. A tearful reunion took place, with Laura repeatedly warning them they'd never be allowed to leave the country again.

And she was getting no argument from them.

He smiled as he finally noticed the young couple's escorts, Dawson, Niner, Atlas, and Spock entering the room then closing the door. It was crowded, but nobody cared as hugs and handshakes and happy greetings were exchanged.

"Sorry about leaving you guys behind," said Dawson. "We were preparing to head back on our own when we got word that Dylan had managed to get himself into position."

Acton squeezed Laura's hand. "Really? We didn't see him."

Dawson jerked a thumb at Reading. "Turns out this one went rogue first, and saved the day."

"What about Jack?" asked Laura. "They took him from the room and we never saw him again."

"Dylan rescued him and got him on a flight to Beijing."

Acton's eyes narrowed. "Isn't that sort of like going from the frying pan to the fire?"

Dawson shrugged. "There are a billion people to lose yourself among in China, and only a few million Mongolians. He's already made contact. He's fine."

"And Dylan?"

"He swung by the hotel and made sure Clarice got out safely—"

Mai cried out. "Oh my God, I forgot about her!"

Dawson chuckled. "Well, not to worry. She's safely on her way home."

"Thank God," sighed Tommy. "I'd have felt horrible. What about those two that were arrested instead of us?"

Dawson frowned. "I'm afraid they've been reported missing by their Chinese parents. I have a feeling it won't be good news."

The room fell silent in honor of two innocents, Laura finally breaking the silence as she wiped a tear away. "And Dylan? Will he be joining us?"

Dawson shook his head. "Nope. Already off on his next assignment as far as I know. That guy is hard to keep track of."

Acton sighed. "Well, I'm happy to hear Dylan and Jack are okay, as well as Clarice. I just wish we had been able to save Arban. That poor kid."

Dawson leaned forward. "Well, I might have something on that."

Acton's chest hammered at Dawson's hopeful tone. "What?"

"Well, apparently that loader that was used to scoop up your Khan guy disappeared from the mine, then reappeared about an hour ago."

Acton smiled as he exchanged an excited glance with Laura. It had to have been Arban. But how? "Does, umm, Langley have any theories?"

"You mean, do they think it was Arban?"

Acton chuckled. "Am I that transparent?"

"They're not making any official comment on it, but from what I gather, the satellite footage shows no evidence of the load it was holding in its bucket being dumped at the mine site, yet when it returned, it was empty."

Laura squeezed Acton's hand. "So, whoever took it, took the remains with them, left it somewhere, then returned the loader so no one would go looking for it."

Acton's head bobbed. "It had to be someone who knew what was in the bucket. A thief would have dumped it right then and there, and then never would have returned."

Tommy interjected. "They might have changed their mind?"

Acton shook his head. "No, they still would have dumped it before leaving the mine site. When we left, there was nobody left behind besides the workers, and none of them knew what was in the bucket. Conrad was in the helicopter with Stander, the rest were either dead or in our helicopter. We assumed Arban was with Stander and Conrad, but when he cut the lights, I know I couldn't see what was going on."

Niner agreed. "I couldn't see anything either. Remember, Stander took his gun off his hostages to shoot out the generator. Arban could have taken that opportunity to escape and lose himself in the dark."

"But why wouldn't he show himself after Stander left?" asked Tommy. "It was safe then."

Acton smiled slightly. "Because he already had a plan. You have to remember that many Mongolians—most—revere Genghis Khan. And Khan's wishes were well-known. He wanted to be buried in his homeland, in an unmarked grave, with no one left to know its location. I think Arban was a true believer, and he took the opportunity to fulfill Khan's wishes once again. I think somewhere out there is a new grave, dug deep once again, with Khan's remains buried, unmarked, where hopefully he's never discovered again."

Tommy frowned. "Well, that's anticlimactic. We should be able to find it, shouldn't we?"

Acton nodded. "Yes, but should we? I mean, haven't the Mongolian people spoken? The soldiers opened fire, killed their own commanding officer, were willing to die to try and protect the gravesite, then the only survivor from the government takes the body and hides it. I think that speaks volumes. If the Mongolians want him found, then they can ask for our help. The surviving soldiers know what was there and I'm sure they've already told their senior officers." He shook his head. "I think we should let Khan rest in peace wherever he now is."

Mai cleared her throat. "He's not exactly the type of man that deserves to rest in peace."

Acton smiled. "Agreed, but, if you believe in such things, then you have to also believe that any punishment he deserved is already being meted out in the next life."

Reading's phone vibrated and he pulled it out, his eyebrows shooting up. "It's a message from Rita Perdok."

Acton's eyes narrowed. "How does she have—oh, right. What's it say?"

"It says, if you see Jim and Laura, I thought they should see this."

"See what?"

"There's a video." He played it, Megadeth's Train of Consequences playing, and Acton smiled, his chest heaving as he knew exactly what would be on the video.

Reading turned the phone so they could see, and tears rolled as he saw his best friend, bandaged head to toe.

With one toe tapping to the beat.

Namjiliin Residence

Ulaanbaatar, Mongolia

Arban frowned at the shattered door jamb. He stepped inside his home tentatively, listening for any signs of intruders, then gasping at the sight. His home had been torn apart, as if whoever had been here had been searching for something with an intentionally destructive ferocity.

Rage filled him for a moment, then satisfaction with the knowledge all those responsible were dead.

And his rage turned to concern.

"Badma?"

There was no answer.

He called out again, louder, and still no answer.

He raced through the small home, checking every room, every closet, every place she might be hiding, or a body might be hidden, and found nothing.

He went to the back door and out into the alleyway behind the row of houses.

"Badma!"

He called several more times before a door opened several homes down.

"Arban?"

His chest heaved with relief as he raced toward her, and she toward him. They slammed into each other, and he held her tight as the tears flowed. He pushed away, holding her face in his hands, his thumbs wiping away her tears, relishing in her beauty as if it had been years since he had last laid eyes upon it.

"Are you okay?"

She nodded, smiling. "Are you?"

He hugged her hard to his chest once again. "Yes, everything is fine."

"Did the professors save you?"

"In a manner of speaking. You met them?"

"They saved me."

"Then I'll have to thank them." They strolled back to their home, arm in arm, saying nothing until they were safely inside.

"What was it all about?"

He stood two chairs upright and they sat facing each other. "We found it."

"What?"

"The tomb. The tomb of Genghis Khan."

Her eyes widened and her mouth opened. "Oh no! What…what will happen?"

"The Shaman's wishes were kept."

She stared at her husband, and he could see the pride. "By you?"

He nodded. "He must forever rest in peace, undisturbed."

"And will he?"

"I've made certain of it."

She smiled. "Then you have done well." She frowned. "Does anyone know? I mean, do they know you did this?"

He chewed his cheek for a moment as he thought. "No, I don't think so, though once Professor Acton discovers I'm alive and the tomb is missing, he'll probably realize it was me."

"That could mean trouble."

He grunted. "Then perhaps we should just let the professor think I'm dead."

"Will that work?"

He shrugged. "I doubt it, but the fact I don't contact him might be enough for him to know I don't want to be asked any questions."

"If word gets out that you might know…"

"Then I'll do what's necessary."

She pulled away. "I don't like the sound of that. You mean—"

He took her hand and patted it. "I'll do whatever is necessary to preserve the secret."

She paled. "You mean…"

He sighed. "I wouldn't be the first to die to preserve the secret. Though I hope I'm the last."

Khentii Region, Mongol Empire

1227 AD

"It is done."

Mutukan frowned. It had taken days, and a toll on the men forced to commit the atrocity. He felt for them all, and thanked the spirits that he had been spared from participating. He sighed. "I regret it was necessary for your men to execute so many of our own."

The general remained stoic. "It was an honor to fulfill the Khan's final wishes."

And that was what Mutukan had to keep reminding himself. All that had taken place was according to his master's wishes. He wanted to be buried in the land of his ancestors, and this was it. He was born less than a day's ride from this very place.

But more importantly, he wanted to be buried where no one would ever find him, and it had been understood from the beginning what that meant.

The only way the secret of his final resting place could be kept was if no one knew.

"I only wish we could have trusted the monks to commit the ultimate sacrifice as your men did, so there would be someone to say the funeral rites over their bodies."

The general's shoulders slumped. "It is unfortunate, though the spirits will take care of their souls, I have no doubt."

Mutukan urged his horse forward as he surveyed the area one last time. The personal guard of a thousand mounted men had executed their orders, eliminating the tens of thousands that had crafted what lay before them—a perfect landscape, with no evidence man had ever disturbed it.

Those same thousand men had ridden their horses repeatedly over the sight of the slaughter, destroying any evidence it had occurred, the river, jammed with bodies, eventually releasing them, those downstream no doubt left to wonder what horrors had taken place. Yet if any were sent to investigate, they would find nothing.

Including the bodies of the personal guard, who had all sacrificed their horses, then themselves, each pushing the next man's body into the river, their general and Mutukan all that remained.

They approached the river and dismounted. Mutukan patted the neck of his horse, one that had served him well for years, then removed any markings, tossing them into the river. He smacked it on its hindquarters, sending it galloping off.

"You're letting him live?"

"I think there's been enough killing of innocents, don't you?"

The general nodded, setting his own horse free. "Almost enough."

Mutukan smiled. "It has been an honor, General."

"The honor has been mine, sir."

Mutukan bowed then stepped into the river, the general following. He drew his dagger and placed it to the general's throat. "Forgive me." He slid it across the skin, slicing it open, the blood flowing freely as the general gasped then slid into the waters, swiftly carried away.

Mutukan closed his eyes, tears flowing as he tilted his head back and placed the knife over his heart.

I will see you soon, my master.

THE END

ACKNOWLEDGMENTS

This book is dedicated to a lovely married couple I've known for years. I won't say why. They know why, and that is all that matters. What is interesting is that Deniz visited me recently with another friend from the past—hey Willy!—and we were talking about my success as a writer. What most don't know is that Deniz is responsible for some of my most popular characters—Bravo Team.

When I wrote The Protocol, I shared it with a few friends to get their feedback, and Deniz was one of them. When he finished the story, he had the courage to tell me what he didn't like about it—that the Bravo Team were automatons.

And he was right.

I had recently read Dan Brown's Deception Point, and it had a Delta Force team in it, and they were all referred to as Delta One, Two, Three, etc. I had copied that style as I figured if it was good enough for one of the biggest selling authors at the time, then it was good enough for me as a first-time novelist.

I was wrong.

Deniz said he wanted to know more about them—names, their backgrounds, what their motivations were.

And on the next draft, Bravo Team was truly born.

Little did I know they'd appear in over thirty books a decade later!

Thanks, Deniz!

As usual, there are people to thank. My dad for all the research, Marc Quesnel for help naming some baddies, Sue Bucksey for some British slang, Brent Richards for some military jargon, and, as usual, my wife, daughter, and mother, as well as the proofing and launch teams.

To those who have not already done so, please visit my website at www.jrobertkennedy.com then sign up for the Insider's Club to be notified of new book releases. Your email address will never be shared or sold, and you'll only receive the occasional email from me, as I don't have time to spam you!

Thank you once again for reading.

Made in the USA
Las Vegas, NV
30 June 2023

74083419R00177